Florence Lean

Phyllida

Vol. 1

Florence Lean

Phyllida
Vol. 1

ISBN/EAN: 9783337342913

Printed in Europe, USA, Canada, Australia, Japan

Cover: Foto ©Andreas Hilbeck / pixelio.de

More available books at **www.hansebooks.com**

PHYLLIDA.

A LIFE DRAMA.

BY

FLORENCE MARRYAT

(Mrs FRANCIS LEAN),

AUTHOR OF 'LOVE'S CONFLICT,' 'MY SISTER THE ACTRESS,'
ETC., ETC., ETC.

IN THREE VOLUMES.

VOL. I.

LONDON: F. V. WHITE & CO.,
31 SOUTHAMPTON STREET, STRAND, W.C.

———

1 8 8 2.

PHYLLIDA.

PROLOGUE.

THE reading of that letter seemed to exhaust Nelson Cole's stock of patience, for before he had finished it he jerked it from his hand, whence it fluttered to the ground.

'Crow away, my bantam!' he said to some imaginary listener, as he lit a cigar and elevated his legs until they formed a right angle with the mantelpiece. 'Crow away! You will have discovered your error

long before you come to my age. Your
theory is all very well *as* a theory, but it
won't wash, my Saint Bernard, it wont
wash.' But after a while spent in watching
the rings of cloudy blue smoke, with which
he was doing his best to fill the apartment,
Nelson Cole seemed to determine that his
friend's letter was too good to lie upon the
floor, for he took the trouble to bring his
legs down to their normal position in order
that he might pick it up, and smooth out its
creased pages on his knee. 'Poor dear
Freshfield,' he thought, somewhat contemptuously as he did so, 'he is a deal
too good for such a naughty world! He
sees no further beyond him than a week-old
puppy. He ought to come to this country
to get his eyes opened. He'd see a few
marriages here and a few women that would
make him view his impossible ideal in its
proper light. How can a man live to eight-
and-twenty and remain so green!'

The letter, as it lay smoothed out on

Nelson Cole's knee (or at least the part that had so much amused him), ran thus :—

'You ask me if I think of marrying again. No ; my dear Cole, that page of my life is, I believe, closed for ever. Not that I have lost the wish or the power to love, far from it—the difficulty is, that in discovering what I have missed, I seemed to have realised a paradise which is too great for attainment. Let me try and explain myself. You know that I married, partly to please my mother, partly to satisfy my conscience. My wife was pretty, amiable, well-bred, and fond of me. We never had a differing word in the course of our married life, and I am sure that she never disregarded a wish that I expressed. Added to all this, I had a tender affection for her, which I still retain for her memory. You will ask me then what more I could desire, and I cannot tell you, excepting this, that our union did not include the union of our souls, and our separation leaves mine still hungering to find its mate. I was fond of poor Alice, and I mourned her loss; but, at the same time, I could have loved fifty other women as well as I loved her, and all at once, if the laws of my country had permitted it.' ('Hullo!' said Nelson Cole, 'here's a nice specimen of an English parson. This is what they call a "muscular Christian," I suppose. Why, the fellow will be wanting to keep a harem next.')

'Now that is not the feeling one should have respecting one's wife. A man should as soon be inclined to be untrue to himself as to her, or to have another self as another wife. Once wedded, should be wedded for eternity, and death should come as a veil only, not as a divorce between man and woman. There should never be a second marriage, Cole; there never *could* be, if the first proved the true union of soul to soul. I have made one mistake, you see, but I will never make another. My eyes have been opened, and the next awakening would

be far more terrible than the first. Of
course my mother will not admit my argu-
ment. She is a good mother to me, but
she holds to the old-fashioned idea that
parsons and doctors should be married men
for the sake of their patients, as if one could
preach truth all the better with a lie in one's
right hand.

'No, Cole! I believe I shall die as I
live, but I shall go through the world with
my eyes open, and should I happily succeed
in finding my soul's mate, whether she be
clothed in rags or satin, seated on a dung-
hill or a throne, I will woo her till she is
mine. But do not imagine that I believe
in the possibility of such happiness—I only
dream of it, as men dream of heaven.'

'Yes! and you may go on dreaming, my
boy,' said Nelson Cole, as he twisted up the
paper, and threw it this time upon the burning fire; 'and you will die dreaming, take
my word for it! Your "soul's mate," indeed!
Show me the women with souls, and I'll

soon find the men to mate with them. But
I question with the followers of Mahomet,
if women have such things. The Lotties
and Dotties and Totties of the present day
go far to persuade us they have not. And
your theory is a dangerous one, Saint Bernard! Going in search of your " soul's mate "
will lead you to wooing your neighbour's
wife perhaps—or striking up a paradisiacal
wedding with your housemaid. I am fond
of this boy with his Puritanical ideas and
close-shorn monkish face, and wish I could
go to England and look after him a bit.
But it can't be just yet, and I must content
myself with a letter of sound practical advice.
The lad was always a dreamer with those
blue eyes and white cheeks of his. Ah!
wait till you come to forty, Bernard, then
you'll know how much a woman is worth
striving for, or grieving after.'

So thinking, our cynical friend reached
down his hat and overcoat, and prepared to
leave the house. He was a sojourner in the

city of Chicago, in the United States of America, at this time; but only for a brief period. His profession, that of a civil engineer, had led him out to the New World some years before, and he had been reaping the golden profits of an experienced hand and clever practical brain ever since. He had been employed in laying down railroads in several of the States, and began to feel himself quite a naturalised American, especially as he was well known, and sure of a welcome in most of their hospitable cities. In Chicago he felt himself peculiarly at home, having many old friends settled there, and as he strolled towards the principal theatre, he knew that he should be met by a score of outstretched hands. And from the male portion of creation, Nelson Cole deserved the cordiality extended to him. He was a man of about fifty—grey-haired, keen-eyed, clear-headed, and critical—a bit of a philosopher without an atom of romance in his composition, and wishing to be thought more

hard and bitter than he naturally was. Es-
sentially a man's man : fond of sport, politics,
late hours, and bachelors' parties, and es-
chewing—like the evil one—all assemblies
where the female element predominated, or
was the principal attraction.

What Nelson Cole really thought of women
few of his own sex had ever heard. He seldom mentioned them ; apparently they engaged his thoughts as little as though they
did not exist. Some men thought that he
must have been cruelly disappointed or
betrayed in his early days : others that he
actually felt as little as he professed to do.
But whatever their speculations, Nelson
Cole remained a thorough good friend and
boon companion to themselves. It was past
eleven o'clock as he entered the theatre
saloon, and the bar was crowded with noisy,
chattering, young men. The babble was
so great, and the discussion so animated,
that his entrance was at first altogether
disregarded, and he had time to gather

some notion of the subject of which they spoke.

'They say he has dismissed her—it's a d—d shame!' cried one.

'I don't see that. I think she fully deserves it. The woman was intoxicated,' replied another.

'Intoxicated!' interrupted a third contemptuously, as though that word were far too weak. 'She was *drunk*—drunk as an owl;' and then the chorus swelled indiscriminately.

'But it's the first time, and it's deuced hard a girl should lose her bread for a single offence.'

'How do you know it's the first time?— not likely. A woman tries it on a good many times in private before she ventures to appear before the public in that condition.'

'Of whom do you speak?' asked Nelson Cole, and then the general attention was diverted to him.

'Oh! here's Cole. How are you, Cole,

old fellow? Glad to see you, my boy!' and so on and so on. But amongst them all Nelson Cole addressed but one.

'Jack Neville!' he exclaimed, 'can I believe my eyes? Where do you hail from? I thought you were safe in San 'Frisco.'

The man he spoke to, a fine, handsome, sun-burned fellow of about thirty, coloured visibly even beneath the tan of a Californian sun.

'Oh, I left 'Frisco long ago, and have been lounging about the South for the last six months,' he replied hurriedly. 'I—I— got into a bit of a scrape down there, you know!'

'And serve you right, my boy, for herding with such a rascal as that Sandie Macpherson,' said Cole. 'I told you what he was from the beginning; and I only hope you've shaken yourself free of his clutches.'

'Be careful, Cole! some one may hear you,' interposed the younger man. 'Macpherson's friend, Pawley, was at the bar not two minutes ago!'

'Pawley may hear me or not,' replied Cole loudly. 'Nothing would give me greater pleasure than to have an opportunity of settling old scores with that detestable Scotch rascal.' But men, as a rule, dislike a disturbance in a public place, especially if it does not concern themselves, and the other loungers at the bar commenced to crowd about Cole, and reiterate the news that had occupied them on his arrival.

'Only fancy, Cole! poor little Stephanie Harcourt.'

'That pretty girl, with the blue eyes and golden hair.'

'Blue eyes, Marshall? What are you talking about? her eyes are as black as night.'

'Black eyes—rubbish! Why, the girl is as fair as she can be.'

'I tell you, her eyes are black, or nearly

so; I've been close to them, and ought to know.'

'Well, well, never mind her eyes!' interrupted Nelson Cole impatiently. What's the matter with the girl?'

'Why, she came in so drunk in the burlesque to-night that she couldn't stand, and Evans has dismissed her from the theatre.'

'That's nonsense! she could *stand* fast enough; only she had had a little too much, and forgot her part.'

'Broke down entirely in her singing, and you know she had *the* song of the evening.'

'Who *is* Stephanie Harcourt?' demanded Cole in an indifferent tone, addressing Jack Neville, who stood next him.

'I don't know,' answered Jack slowly, as he moved away.

'She's quite a beginner — only been on the boards a few months—and I think it's awfully hard lines on her to get her dismissal for a little mistake,' said another young man. Nelson Cole's hard voice fell like cold water on his enthusiasm.

'Drunkenness is never a little mistake with women : when they once begin, they go on, and Evans is quite right to check the first symptoms of it by a summary dismissal. He'll find plenty of girls to take Miss Harcourt's place. There are more than enough of them in the world, heaven knows.'

'You didn't expect to get any sympathy out of Cole, I suppose?' laughed some of the men at the drinking-bar, as the person they spoke of elbowed his way from amongst them, and went to the private room of his old friend, the manager, where, after a little desultory conversation, he contrived to bring the subject round to Miss Stephanie Harcourt's offence.

'Sorry to hear you had a *fracas* on the boards to-night, Evans.'

'Yes, a disgraceful business! Little Harcourt perfectly intoxicated! I was rather afraid of it from the beginning. She's a strangely excitable girl.'

' Got connections in Chicago ? '

' Don't know, I'm sure. I've heard some report of her being married, but I don't trouble myself about the affairs of my company outside the theatre. But I was obliged to make an example of her. I had no end of trouble last year with a woman named Harrison, who went on in the same way, so I gave Miss Harcourt her dismissal then and there.'

' Shall you miss her ? '

' Not much. She's a sharp girl, but no particular talent, and I fancy she'll not find it easy to get employment on the boards again in *this* city.'

' Not when you've made a public example of her from your theatre, certainly,' replied Nelson Cole, with apparently the utmost indifference to Stephanie Harcourt's fate. Yet the girl's pathetic eyes and mouth, which he had noticed but cursorily in his visits to the Athenian Theatre, seemed to haunt him strangely for the remainder of the evening, and when he rose to return home, he passed out by the stage door and asked the porter if he knew Miss Harcourt's address.

'I can't say I do, sir; but I think that lady can tell us. Miss Vavasour,' he continued, addressing a tall, closely-veiled figure about to cross the threshold, 'can you tell this gentleman where Miss Harcourt lives?'

The veiled woman turned, and regarded Nelson Cole somewhat suspiciously.

'She lives with me,' she replied, with caution; 'do you wish to send her a message?'

'Are you her friend?' asked Nelson Cole, stepping out into the street beside her.

'I am, sir. Are you?'

'I should wish to be, Miss Vavasour! I feel for the misfortune that has overtaken her this evening, and if she requires assistance—it is a delicate thing that I would say, but perhaps you understand me—'

' It is a kind thing, sir,' replied the actress, they were walking slowly on together by this time, 'and in her name I thank you for it. Her dismissal from the Athenian is a very serious matter, for she has no other means of support, but I hope she may get work some-how. You mustn't think this is a habit with her, sir—indeed—indeed—it is the first time she has ever so transgressed. I have known her for eighteen months, and I can swear to it; but Mr Evans would not take my word.'

' And what was the occasion of this first transgression, Miss Vavasour? Do you know?'

' I am not sure if I should be justified in disclosing Stephanie's secrets, sir; but she has had great trouble. I can tell you so much, and an old friend met her out to-day and told her some good news, and took her in and treated her to dinner somewhere, and I think it was the load off her mind and the excitement and the champagne altogether that did it.'

'Poor child! no wonder it had an effect upon her. But what will she do now for a living?'

'I don't know, sir! You had better ask Stephanie herself. It is here that we live together. This is our door!'

'Thank you for the information. Of course I cannot intrude to-night, but to-morrow perhaps, if you would prepare Miss Harcourt for my appearance—'

But he had not had time to finish his sentence before the door of the house was thrown open, and Stephanie Harcourt appeared upon the threshold.

'Bella,' she cried to her friend hysterically, 'it is all over. I am dismissed without salary, and I can't even pay you my share of the week's rent! The sooner I go to the Tombs with that scoundrel the better!'

'Hush, hush, dear! there is a stranger present,' said Miss Vavasour compassionately.

But the girl was too excited to heed her caution.

'I might have known misfortune was at hand,' she went on passionately, 'for I met *him* to-day, you know who I mean—my evil genius. There has always been trouble for me following in the wake of Sandie Macpherson.'

At that name, heard for the second time that evening, Nelson Cole started ; but he was too much a man of the world not to conceal his surprise.

'Stephanie! this gentleman wishes to be your friend, but this is not the time for you to speak to him. Come in now and let us go to bed, and to-morrow, when you are more composed, perhaps he will come and hear the story of your troubles,' said Miss Vavasour.

'I shall never be more composed,' replied the girl incoherently. I have had so little good luck in my life. Why couldn't they have left me the little I possessed. But now

I've lost everything, and I might just as well be in the Tombs with him as starving in the streets of Chicago. Oh, those horrid dreary Tombs! Why did I ever meet Jack?'

'Come in, come in,' whispered her friend, in a soothing voice.

Nelson Cole tried to make his escape without further parley.

'I will call to-morrow afternoon,' he said, as he lifted his hat and turned away.

'Do you know Sandie Macpherson?' screamed Stephanie after him, and that name from her lips seemed somehow to send a chill through him.

What connection this poor little burlesque actress in Chicago could possibly have with the desperate and evil-disposed gold-digger of Sacramento Valley, whose villainy had cast a secret shadow over his own life, he could not imagine; but the fact of her having mentioned his name would have drawn him to her side again, without the inducement of wishing to befriend her poverty. He tried to persuade himself, in his free and easy manner, that the whole affair troubled him but little ; but the fact is that it troubled him very much, to the extent of preventing his going to sleep till the early morning, and not waking up until it was time to keep his appointment with Miss Harcourt. But when he reached her presence, it was a very different person who presented herself to him from the flushed and dishevelled Bacchante of the day before. It was a very pale and miserable-looking girl—half frightened and half ashamed—whom Miss Vavasour dragged rather than led into the room to be introduced to him. There was none of the brazen defiance of a woman used to vice in Stephanie Harcourt.

She looked rather like a child who had been detected in some fault and brought up for punishment.

She knew now what had befallen her the night before ; and it was so terrible to be presented to this grave, elderly man, who

had seen her a prey to the most disgusting
vice of which a woman can be guilty. But
the worldly view that Nelson Cole took of
the matter reassured her. If he had looked
shocked, the girl would have shrunk from
his scrutiny. Had he sympathised with her,
she would have broken down,—but he treated
it as a matter of every-day occurrence, as indeed it unfortunately was with the women he
was most in the habit of seeing.

'Come, come, Miss Harcourt,' he said,
as she held backward, 'this has been an unfortunate accident ; but accidents will happen,
as we all know, in the best regulated families.
You will not be surprised to hear that your
face is well known to me, as it is to most
of the inhabitants of Chicago, and perhaps
your friend here, Miss Vavasour, has told
you that if I can be of any assistance to
you in this dilemma, I will. I am an old
man, you see, and you need have no scruples
in accepting my help. What can I do for
you ?'

'Can you get me other work?' demanded the girl shyly.

'Perhaps I can. At all events I will try. What do you wish to do? Do you intend to apply for another engagement in Chicago?'

'Oh no; anything but that—anything but that,' cried Stephanie, with visible repugnance. 'I could not bear the shame of another public appearance here. If there were only work that I could do to be procured in the country—in the open peaceful country.'

'Do you love the country, then?'

'Oh! to find oneself there,' continued the girl excitedly. 'To wake up and find oneself amongst the primroses and violets, and the cool, cool grass, and the leafy trees and waving corn, and to know that one had done for ever with the noise and glare of the town, and the cruel bricks and mortar that seem to press upon one's heart, and keep all the joy and freshness of life from bubbling over.'

'Stephanie, do think what you are saying!' exclaimed Miss Vavasour. 'The gentleman asked you what work you would like best. You must excuse her wandering, sir,' she continued to Nelson Cole, 'for she is still weak and feverish, and I don't think she half knows what she is talking about.'

'Pray, let her talk as she will—I am interested in all she can tell me,' he replied; and, indeed, a colder man than himself must needs have felt some interest in the ultimate fate of the beautiful creature before him. For Stephanie Harcourt was beautiful, with more than the mere physical beauty of colour and shape. She was about eighteen years of age, with a graceful figure of middle height—a head of rippling golden hair— whether natural or artifical Nelson Cole was not skilled enough to determine, and pathetic eyes of some deep neutral tint, which looked just now like the eyes of a hunted animal. But her greatest charm lay in the far-off look of those eyes, as if her soul saw more 'that was presented to her earthly vision, and was filled with high and glowing thoughts. As Nelson Cole gazed upon those upturned eyes, they reminded him of—he knew not what—and he turned away with a shudder.

'Have you ever lived in the country, Miss Harcourt?' he asked her presently.

'No! no! Never! I have been reared amongst the glare and the gas of cities. I can remember nothing but the smell of liquor and the sound of oaths, and the clash of the dice and the billiard balls, and the horrid, horrid bricks and mortar.'

'You must have had a strange experience?'

'Ah! you would say so if you knew all I have passed through before I came to Chicago—all the horrors that I saw in San Francisco. How I wish,' she went on passionately, 'that that place and every-thing connected with it, down to its very name, might be burned off the face of the earth!'

'You mustn't excite youself like this,' said Nelson Cole. 'It is giving way to their feelings after that fashion that makes people forget themselves, as you did yesterday.'

'But that was an accident—indeed it was! How could I imagine a little wine would affect me so? And Jack said it would do me good. And we laughed and talked so much I did not notice how often he filled my glass, and I felt so well and happy until I walked out of the keen frosty air into the theatre, and then, somehow, all the lights seemed to close round me, and my head felt like a feather, and I seemed to be float-ing somewhere between the flies and the stage, until a crash came and I fell down. But it was all Jack's fault. He ought not to have given me so much champagne.'

'Is Jack your husband?'

'Who told you I had a husband?'

'You see I know it.'

'Ah! and so you may! Every one may know it now, if they choose, for it can't last long. Jack my husband! Oh no! he's only a friend; but we came across each other yesterday in the streets, and he gave me news of him that drove me mad.'

' Not mad with grief, I hope.'

' No! no! mad with joy? And what do you think the news was? That he's locked up for two years in the Tombs for forgery. Two years! Two long, blessed years. And I shall be free before he comes out, Bella, sha'n't I?' she cried, as she cast herself into the arms of her friend. ' Free from him and from all of them. Free to bury my secrets in the sea; free from that awful curse—'

' Hush, dear, don't talk so fast. Yes, yes, you shall be free, if there's any justice or truth in the laws of our country. But, meanwhile, you must live, you know, and this gentleman is kind enough to say that he will help you, and I do think if he would assist you to go to your friends for a little while, and try and forget all this misery before you turn your thoughts to work again, that it would be the kindest thing he could do.'

'Never fear,' said Nelson Cole, 'but that I will perform all that I have promised. Meanwhile, Miss Harcourt, your disclosures have interested me very much. May I ask the name of your husband?'

'Oh yes; it is no secret. He is a Brazilian, called Fernan Cortës.'

'And—pardon me, he is a rascal!'

'The greatest rascal that ever existed, sir.'

'My poor child, how came you to marry him?'

'I can't tell you that. I was frightened into it in a way that you would hardly understand. Only, thank heaven, I am now delivered from him.'

'But after his two years' incarceration are over, he will come out again and claim you.'

'I will have broken the chain by that time. I will have gone far away where he shall never find me.'

'And you met Cortës in San Francisco?'

'Yes, sir.'

'And that scoundrel Sandie Macpherson had some hand in your marrying him?'

The girl's cheek became as white as ashes.

'Who has told you that?'

'No one. I guessed it.'

'You have guessed wrong, sir. But I hate Macpherson. God forgive me. I hate him like my life.'

'You share the feeling with many others. He is a man universally detested.'

'But few know him as I do,' murmured the girl; 'all his cruelty, his artifice, his secret crimes. And my poor mother—can I ever forget her?'

'He injured your mother too?'

'Ah, sir, do not ask me to speak of it! Whom has he not injured? But when you hear me talk of the peace and quiet of the country, as if I were talking of heaven, remember that I can never disassociate the rattle and bustle and glare of the town from the thought of cruelty and crime.'

Nelson Cole left his seat and began to pace up and down the room.

'Did you live long in California?' he asked.

' Many years. All my life, until I came here.'

' Did you ever happen to meet there,—a a—anybody of the name of Summers?'

'A woman?' inquired Stephanie innocently.

' Yes ; yes ; well—a—a—woman.'

'No; I never knew any woman there except my mother, till she died.'

'And you said yesterday that you had seen Sandie Macpherson in this town?'

' Oh yes, sir; I met him suddenly,' with a shudder ; ' but he did not see me, and so I escaped him.'

'One would think from the way you mention him, that this man had a hold on you, Miss Harcourt.'

Stephanie glanced meaningly at her friend before she answered.

‘No—not a hold—only—I am afraid of him.’

‘And you would like to get far away from all the places where you are likely to meet him again ? ’

‘ Ah ! so much—so much ! ’

‘ Well, I will put you in the way of doing so. There ; no thanks. I have more money than I know what to do with myself—and if a few dollars can benefit you, you are welcome to them. But I suppose you ought to know my name. I am Nelson Cole the engineer, and you shall hear from me again in the course of the day.’

So saying, this eccentric man, without a single glance of admiration at the beautiful girl, who was sitting with her head bowed in her hands like a repentant Magdalen, seized his hat, and with a curt ‘ Good afternoon,’ left the two women by themselves. And as he returned to his hotel, he was ready to laugh at himself for a fool for having been taken in by swollen eyelids and a downcast countenance.

'What is this girl to me,' he thought impatiently, as he traversed the streets, 'that I should offer to throw away my money upon her? A trumpery little burlesque actress who chooses to disgrace herself by drinking champagne with any Jack who invites her to celebrate with him her husband's arrest for forgery. And I must needs put my finger in the pie and offer to provide her with liquor for the next six months. I am a fool, and no mistake. And yet there is something in the child's voice and look that attracts me in spite of myself. I don't believe she can be all bad ; however, appearances are against her. Well, I've done the job now, and I can't draw back from it. I'll send her a bill for two hundred dollars to-morrow, and wash my hands of the whole affair.'

For the names of San Francisco and

Sandie Macpherson rankled more in Nelson Cole's mind than all the troubles of Stephanie Harcourt. They had raised up the old bull-dog feeling in his breast, which for years he had attempted to quell by never mentioning the man whom he hated, nor thinking of him more than was absolutely necessary.

Yet here he was in the same town as himself, and Nelson Cole felt as if it were impossible for him to sleep until they had met, and had it out with one another.

But an excellent dinner had the power to soothe much of his resentment, and when it was concluded, he prepared, as usual, to finish up his evening at the theatre.

As he was putting the finishing touch to his attire before the mirror, some thought of Bernard Freshfield's last letter suddenly struck him, and he burst into a loud laugh.

'Oh, my saintly parson, with the impossible theory,' he exclaimed, 'you should see the end of a few of the marriages that are made

in heaven before you attempt to foist your
ideas of an eternal union on the world.
The ignoramus! why, his marriage with his
Alice — innocent, inoffensive, and quickly
brought to an end—*was* the true ideal had
he only known it! Where will he ever find
such another wife—to live with him peace-
ably for two years, and leave him a free
man at the end of them? He has had the
luck of one in a thousand. Yet he con-
tinues to whine after the true soul union.
Bosh! What would he say if he could see
poor little Harcourt getting tipsy for joy,
because her husband is locked up for two
years, or knew of—of—a dozen other cases
I could name where men have commenced
their married lives with passionate con-
gratulations, and ended them by cursing
all mankind?

'My Saint Bernard decidedly wants his
eyes opened for him, and they'll be opened
some day by a woman of a different type
from his beautified Alice.

'Well, well—it matters little. The only question is, whether it is possible to save a man from such suffering, or desirable to save him if it were possible. We must all live and learn. But the man who theoretically places woman on such a high pedestal as Freshfield does, is sure to find out his mistake. Woman was never meant for a pedestal. She is out of our reach there; we want her in our arms. Consequently madam has to be pulled down and show her feet of clay. If we could only be content to worship them from a distance, or keep them under a glass-shade, how long they would last. But I mustn't forget my promise to the poor child, who tumbled so unmistakably from her little pedestal last night.'

So saying he enclosed a bill for two hundred dollars in an envelope, addressed to Miss Harcourt, and strolled off to the theatre, as if he had never done a kind action in his life. He searched eagerly there for Jack Neville, but he was nowhere to be seen.

'Jack Neville!' exclaimed an old Chicago man, who knew everything and everybody. 'You wont meet him here to-night, my boy. He's levanted to the South again ; went off like a shot directly he heard a rumour that that old black-leg Macpherson was in the town.'

'And quite right of him too,' said another voice. 'Neville's burnt his fingers once in the company of Sandie Macpherson, and the less he's seen with him in the future the better.'

'Well, he needn't have been in such a blazing hurry with respect to Sandie this time,' interposed a third speaker, 'for the old man wasn't twenty-four hours in the town, and only passed through on his way from New York.'

'Is he gone again?' demanded Nelson Cole.

'That is so, sir. Sandie Macpherson is

not the man to stay where he isn't sure of a welcome, and he is too well known to our force to be able to walk the streets of Chicago with any comfort by daylight. So he showed his sense by making tracks, sir, as soon as his business with us was concluded.'

'It is as well, perhaps, for him that he has,' replied Nelson Cole; and the subject was dropped amongst them. A few days after, a lurking desire to learn Stephanie Harcourt's plans, and to assure her that Chicago was delivered from the presence of her enemy, led him again to the actress's door, where he was met by Miss Vavasour alone.

'Oh, Mr Cole!' she exclaimed, 'I have been longing to see you, or to leave your address that I might deliver Stephanie's thanks to you for your goodness and generosity.'

'She received my letter, then?'

'Indeed, she did. It conveyed new life to her. She left Chicago the very next day!'

'She has left already! You surprise me. Where has she gone?'

'That I cannot tell you, for I do not know myself. I agreed with Stephanie, that since her desire is to lose herself in a new name and a new existence, that it was best no one should share the secret. Oh! she has suffered terribly, sir; her young life has been a chapter of horrors. You have done a most benevolent action in aiding her to escape from its consequences!'

'I hope she may escape them, but I question if it is possible. Anyway, she is safely out of the city, and has friends, I suppose, to go to?'

'Yes, sir; she has connections, I believe, on the mother's side, with whom she can find a refuge. But I must not forget the packet she left for you.'

She went to a drawer and produced thence a tiny parcel tied up in paper, and directed to himself. He opened it. It contained an ordinary wedding-ring, and these words :—

'Dear Friend,—I am too poor to give you anything but my thanks. But keep this! It was my mother's wedding-ring. It is my best possession. It will remind you sometimes that I was not ungrateful for your goodness. Stephanie.'

'Rubbish!' exclaimed Nelson Cole roughly; 'what did the girl mean by leaving me this? What does she suppose I can want with her mother's wedding-ring?'

'It was all she had, sir,' said Miss Vavasour mildly; 'and she was very grateful for your kindness to her.'

'Stuff and nonsense! You shouldn't have allowed it. Can't you send it back to her?'

'I do not know her address.'

'She will write to you.'

'I do not think so. I think she has gone away from us for ever.'

'Well, I suppose I must keep it; but it

was an absurd idea on the girl's part. What the d—l am I to do with somebody else's wedding-ring ?'

He shoved it awkwardly in his waistcoat pocket as he spoke, and having wished Miss Vavasour good-day, turned into the street again. He would not have confessed the fact to himself, nor any other control for the world ; but he felt quite disappointed to find that Stephanie Harcourt had left Chicago without wishing him good-bye, or leaving any trace of her destination.

And when he reached home he transferred the little scrap of paper and the old wedding-ring carefully to a safe corner of his dispatch box, where they could neither be discovered nor disturbed.

And then Nelson Cole went on his way through the busy hard-working world, and except for an occasional remembrance that made him smile rather than sigh, he forgot all about his adventure with the little actress in the city of Chicago.

CHAPTER I.

IT was a bright, beautiful afternoon in the height of summer—not a miserable, humbugging, makeshift for a summer, such as we have had for the last ten years, but a real, good, old-fashioned one, like those that Adam and Eve enjoyed in Paradise, before rain and cold joined league with the other curses of mankind to come out of their proper season. This had been and was still a glorious time, when all the fragrant essences of grass and herbs were drawn out by the hot sun, and perfumed the land long after he had sunk to rest, when the tangled blossoms rioted

over the flower-beds in the profusion of
their bearing, and the branches of the fruit
trees and bushes, over-weighted, hung to
the ground, and the earth was warm and
dry from early morn to dewy eve.

The noble acacias on the lawn of Blue
Mount formed leafy bowers of themselves,
and under the shade of one of them, in her
ordinary dress, without fear of the exposure,
sat Mrs Freshfield knitting. Mrs Freshfield was always knitting. No one ever
encountered her sitting or standing on a
week-day without a huge ball of worsted
and two or four large wooden pins in her
hands. What she manufactured, or what
became of the products of her labour, remained a mystery. The shelves of her
mahogany wardrobe were piled with pounds
of wool of various colours, which gradually
became drawn into the general web and
disappeared, to be replaced by more; but
where it went to in the form of stitches
Mrs Freshfield seemed unable to account

for. Her daughter Laura declared she made
petticoats for old sinners, who sold them as
fast as they received them, so that each
pensioner wore out about half-a-dozen in
the course of twelve months. But Mrs Freshfield was strictly pious, and in the habit of
sternly repressing Laura's profane jests.
She had not been a young woman when
she married her late husband, John Freshfield, the Sheffield merchant, who bought
Blue Mount and its surroundings as a retreat for his old age. Mrs Freshfield had
been extremely pious even in those days,
but her piety had not prevented her marrying the Sheffield merchant on account of
his money.

Surely we have seen such things in the
world before. A golden bait is almost as
irresistible to the elect as to the ungodly—
only they call their temptation by a different name. Mrs Freshfield thought that
Mr Freshfield's riches would prove such a
snare to him that he would require a help-

meet like herself to counteract their evil influence. She married him to convert him (so she said), but she never succeeded in doing so, for he died as hardened an old sinner as he had lived, begging his physician with his last breath to keep his wife and her cant out of his room. Thus deprived of the triumph of making a saint of her husband, Mrs Freshfield turned her attention to her children. There were two of them — Bernard and Laura, and although they were young people who dared to think for themselves in certain matters, they had certainly so far profited by their mother's training, that the young man was pure and refined and religious in his ideas to a degree, extraordinary in this age of free thought and unbridled actions ; and the girl, though light-hearted and full of fun, was as delicate and modest as any English girl could be.

Mrs Freshfield was an old woman. She had numbered nearly forty years when Bernard was born to her, and he was now past eight-and-twenty, and from the first she had always destined this unlooked-for blessing to the ministry of the church. Bernard had been brought up from an infant with the knowledge that he was to be a parson, and a parson he had consequently become. His father had left him ample means, and he had no need to work; but it was his mother's wish, and he never dreamt of disputing it. Perhaps he sometimes regretted that he had yielded so easily; he had his own thoughts and ideas about a parson's duty, and they clashed occasionally with the rules set down for him; but, if so, he did not express his regrets openly, but laboured as faithfully as he could for the good of the inhabitants of Bluemere.

He did not live with his mother. On the occasion of his marriage he had taken a smaller but very pretty house about half-a-mile from the Mount, and he continued to occupy it and to keep a kennel of sporting dogs, which shocked Mrs Freshfield—and a couple of hunters, which horrified her still more. Indeed, the greatest calamities of her life were, that Bernard *would* wear a velveteen coat in the mornings and would *not* give up smoking. To be a smoking, hunting, shooting parson in a velveteen coat seemed, in poor Mrs Freshfield's narrow mind, very much like selling oneself to the devil ; but still Bernard was a good son to her, and she was a good mother to him, and so they managed to get on together, notwithstanding that on some points he would have his own way. A mother must not hope to exercise any influence but that of love over a son of eight-and-twenty, who possesses a couple of thousand a-year in his own right, and will come into all her property when she dies. But Bernard had always been Mrs Freshfield's favourite child, and as she watched him coming across the lawn to her that afternoon, the old lady's eyes glistened and her hands trembled with the pleasure of seeing him again. For Laura

was absent too, and she had the prospect
of having the conversation with him all to
herself, a pleasure she seldom enjoyed.

Bernard came up to his mother and greeted
her affectionately. This young fellow, already a widower at eight-and-twenty, had
a heart brimming over with love for all
who loved him. He was not particularly
good-looking—no one would have called
him an Antinous or a Hercules, but he
had a straight athletic figure—a kind, honest
face, and blue eyes that were peculiarly
tender and earnest in their expression. His
widowhood had not sat very heavily upon
his spirits, and he had never pretended it
had done so ; but it had left a quiet subdued
demeanour behind it, that was particularly
noticeable when he was alone. Then he
often sighed and heavily—not because his
bereavement had bereaved him so much,
but because it had bereaved him so little.
He sighed for himself, because he seemed
to have gained something where he had

really lost, and it made him realise how little he had ever possessed. He was a strange young man, as these pages will show ; but he was honest to himself withal.

'Bernard, my dear,' said Mrs Freshfield, with some little show of excitement, 'we are to have guests to-morrow. The Muck-heeps have been in London for a month, and are coming to spend a few weeks at Blue Mount before they return to Scotland.'

'Indeed, mother ! I hope you'll feed them up well. They look as if they needed it— or at all events Miss Janet does.'

'Now, Bernard, my dear, I call that a very unkind speech on your part, and quite unbefitting your calling. It would lead one to think that you value your friends on account of their money or money's worth. If the Misses Muckheep—notwithstanding their good old blood—are not as wealthy as ourselves, it is their misfortune and not their fault.'

Mrs Freshfield delivered the phrase

'good old blood' with an unctuous smack, for, be it known, this very pious lady, who professed to despise the wealth of which she had a superfluity, cherished an over-whelming weakness for 'blood,' which was the only thing money could not buy for her, and would have given much to see her son contract a second alliance with some woman of 'family.'

But the Reverend Bernard did not seem to notice the maternal rebuke. His ear had been caught by another sentence.

' I wish, mother,' he said, as he took a seat beside her, 'that you would not speak of everything as either befitting or unbe-fitting my "*calling*." The term is one that grates upon me. It insinuates that I had a spiritual call to undertake the work of a minister, and you know that I had no such thing. I became a parson because you urged me to the step, and wished to keep me by your side, and I entered the profession with far too little sense of its responsibilities.'

'Bernard, you don't mean to tell me that you regret it?' exclaimed Mrs Freshfield with horror.

'No, dear mother, I do not! Had I to choose over again, I might draw back from undertaking so much more than I feel myself able to perform; but as the duty has been pressed upon me, I will discharge it as faithfully as I can. Only don't try to make me out better than I am. Let me work amongst my sick and suffering people in my own way, and comfort them with a friend's sympathy and advice, but don't set me up as an example of piety and virtue, because that you know I am not.'

'Bernard! I am sure that you are all that is best and most praiseworthy. Mrs Pinner was saying, only the other day, that the life you lead is an example to any young man.'

'I am much obliged to Mrs Pinner for her opinion, but I should hardly think that her experience enhanced the value of her recommendation, and I don't think that a parson should be set up as a little oracle amongst his people. It is the truth he preaches that should be worshipped—not himself. What, am I not a man like all the rest of them ? '

' Oh, Bernard, my dear, don't say that,' murmured his mother deprecatingly.

' A man with all the tastes and feelings of a man,' he went on, 'and with no notion that I sin in indulging any taste that is not contrary to law. If hunting and shooting and dancing and smoking are sinful, then they are sinful for everybody as well as for me, and we must all renounce them as evil habits. But if they are innocent for my parishioners, then they are equally innocent for myself. And yet I know I shock you, my dear mother, and many other estimable people by these worldly proclivities of mine, and you think I can neither go to heaven myself, nor teach my people the way there, unless I systematically look as if I were bound for the other place !'

'Oh, my dear Bernard, but then your sacred calling—'

'There you go again, mother! my "calling,"' said Bernard, as he rose to his feet and walked up and down the grass. 'I tell you if anybody "called" me to the ministry, it was yourself, and I am not going to make what may prove a harmless matter into a very evil one, by living a life false to myself and to my own notions of right, out of prejudice to the opinions of the world.'

'Well, well, my dear boy, pray sit down again and don't excite yourself in this needless manner. I don't know what I can have said to raise such a discussion. But the fact is, Bernard, the house is lonely to you since your great misfortune, and you don't care to stay at home as you ought to do. When are you going to dispel the shadow, my son, and brighten your home again. It seems quite unnatural, not to say wrong, to me, that a minister should remain unmarried?'

'Why so?'

But to this plain question Mrs Freshfield seemed puzzled to find an answer.

'I can tell you, mother. . Because you think the vows a man makes to heaven are weaker than those he makes to a woman, and that though the latter may keep him in the straight and narrow path, he is not to be trusted to remain faithful to the former.'

'My dear Bernard, you really do say such things.'

'I only put your thoughts into words. It was with that idea that you threw me into the society of poor Alice, and persuaded me she was breaking her heart on my account, until I thought it was my duty to marry the girl, and tell the first lie that had ever passed my lips before God's altar.'

'Bernard, Bernard, it shocks me beyond

measure to hear you speak in this manner, and of such a dear, good loving wife as she made you too.'

'I say nothing against her, poor girl; God forbid I should. But as far as I was concerned, that marriage was a blasphemy and a sacrilege—a blasphemy against love and a sacrilege of the highest human sacrament that God designed for the regeneration of mankind.'

'Well, I can't say I follow you, my dear. She was a sweet girl, and you made her an excellent husband, and what more could anybody desire?'

Bernard's quiet eyes were fixed upon the sky, glowing with the first glories of sunset.

'I don't know if she felt the void,' he said, in a low voice, 'but I wanted—completion.'

'Oh dear! oh dear!' exclaimed Mrs Freshfield, dropping stitches by the dozen in her perplexity. 'I don't understand all

these new-fangled terms, but I know what
I want, Bernard, and that is to see you
happily settled again, and my little grand-
children toddling about my knees, before
I am called home to join your father.'

'Dear old mother,' replied the young man
affectionately, as he laid his hand upon hers,
'it is a very natural wish, and I hope it
may be gratified.   But would not Laura
do as well for the agent of such happiness
as myself?'

'*Laura!*' ejaculated Mrs Freshfield em-
phatically. 'No—not at all.   In the first
place, Laura's children could never be the
same to me as yours, Bernard.   They would
not be Freshfields ; and in the second, a
girl can't marry when she chooses, and a
man can.'

'Oh, that is only a mother's partiality,'
laughed her son, 'and I am afraid the
marriageable young ladies of Bluemere would
not be disposed to record your assertion.'

'Nonsense, Bernard!   There are a dozen

in Bluemere alone who would jump at you.'

' Let me hear the roll-call, mother. Who knows but what I might take a fancy to one or two of them.'

Mrs Freshfield bridled with importance. She really thought her son was beginning to look at the matter in a practical light.

' Well, my dear, there is Mrs Norman She is not older than yourself, and her father's cousin is the Earl of Carisborough !'

' Mrs Norman ! The pretty widow at Willow Cottage ? No, no, mother, she paints !'

' Only on occasions, Bernard ; and you could soon break her off that.'

' She wont do, I tell you. It is of no use.'

' Miss Warrender. You have often re-marked how handsome she is.'

' The sorrowful lady with a secret in her life ? Mrs Bernard Freshfield's former life must contain no secrets, mother. It must be open to inspection as the light of day.'

'You can have no such objection to make to Nellie Palmer.'

'Pretty little, timid, bashful Nellie. I am afraid she's too shy for me. Those girls who can never look you straight in the face are invariably flirts when your back is turned.'

'Annie Warren, then, who was our poor Alice's bosom friend, and nursed her like a sister in her last illness. Her chief pleasure lies in the parish work, Bernard, and I am sure she loves you already.'

'And for that very reason I would never make her my wife. Dear little charitable Bluemere would say at once that we had settled the matter over Alice's dying bed. No, mother, none of these women will do to fill the vacant place, and I have only been having a little pleasantry with you in even talking of them. I shall never marry again. I feel sure of it, because I see no chance of meeting the woman whom I could love.'

' Not if you continue to be so fastidious,' replied his mother, vexed at finding he had only been in jest. ' But I suppose we may depend upon seeing you at dinner to-morrow to welcome our guests. You know what a dear, good creature Miss Muckheep is, and what a hearty interest she takes in everything that concerns your calling.'

' Yes, yes,' cried Bernard hastily, as he jumped to his feet. ' If you wish it, I will be here.'

' Of course I wish it, and Bella too ; such a sweet, unaffected girl, without the least pride about her, although her father, the Laird of Muckheep, can trace his ancestors back to the time of the Picts and Scots.'

' Just so, when they were a party of untamed savages, and wore nothing but skins, if so much. I hope Miss Bella is a little more civilised than she was on the occasion of her last visit here, for I remember thinking her a terrible Goth.'

'My dear Bernard, her aunt writes me word that she is everything that is most charming, and imbued with the deepest religious feeling.'

'She will be an excellent companion for Laura, then, who is certainly not imbued with too much. I don't believe the monkey would ever come to church except for the pleasure of seeing me!'

'And you encourage her in it, Bernard; deeply as I regret to say it, Laura would certainly be more attentive to her religious duties if you spoke with more severity against her neglect of them.'

'And make the duties as hateful in her eyes as I should become myself. Would you have me set up as an ogre or janitor to my only sister, instead of a loving friend? No, mother, I cannot do it. Let Laura follow her own inclinations. An unwilling sacrifice can never be acceptable.'

'Well, my dear, I cannot help thinking you are far too lax in your ideas, and I wish you had a dear, good partner to consult with you on all these knotty points.'

'Good-bye, mother, you shall see me at dinner to-morrow,' exclaimed Bernard, as he turned away and walked rapidly across the lawn, fearful lest another minute's conversation might renew the vexed question of a second wife.

CHAPTER II.

AS he retraced his steps towards Briarwood (as his own house was called), followed by a couple of setters and a greyhound, his face was more thoughtful than usual. For notwithstanding Mrs Freshfield's doubts and his own modesty, this young man felt more deeply than he cared to acknowledge the responsibilities of the post he had undertaken. He earnestly desired to show a good example to the people under his charge, and to advise them profitably on the best means of regulating their lives; but the difficulty with Bernard Freshfield

was to make up his own mind as to which
was the best example and the best way.
He knew, of course, that a pure and charitable and useful life was obligatory on all
who called themselves Christians; but it
was in the smaller matters, in the petty
laws laid down by custom, the rules observed because everybody else observes
them, the thousand and one fretting obliga-
tions imposed upon men by disciplinarians,
lest a 'brother should offend,' that Bernard
Freshfield hesitated to do more than tell
his parishioners to judge for themselves. He
had seen certain parsons, in their endeavours
to drive men like a flock of sheep to heaven,
afraid to dance or sing, or join in merriment
of any kind, and he knew how futile those endeavours had proved, to do more than make
their fellow-creatures hypocrites. He had
watched these ministers, setting themselves
up as gods amongst the people, and arrogat-
ing to themselves the power they deprecated
in those of another faith, of refusing com-

munion, or marriage, or burial to the persons
whom they, in their finite wisdom, deemed
unworthy of such privileges. And he had
marked how their refusals had hardened the
hearts they should have melted, and drawn
down curses on their own heads instead of
blessings.

He had seen parsons who frowned openly
with the world at the wife's adultery, the
maid-servant's seduction, the apprentice's
theft ; pass over (also with the world) the
master's dishonest dealing, the gentleman's
fornication, the fast woman's coquetry, and
the mistress's ill temper, because they were
unrecognised sins, and they did not feel they
had any right to meddle with them. Bernard Freshfield did not play parson on this
wise. Where he saw what appeared to him
to be wrong, he spoke openly, whether it
was to poor little Jack with a dirty head,
playing at pitch - and - toss with a stolen
halfpenny on Sunday, instead of going to
school ; or to the squire's son, lounging

about his father's park on the same day, with
bloodshot eyes and aching head, cheerful
reminiscences of his debauch of the night before; and whatever fault Bernard found himself called upon to tackle, he always had a
pleasant way of making the offender understand that if he had not committed the same
sin himself, he most likely would have done
so under similar circumstances, until the
humbled heart felt that, given the resolution
and the opportunity, it might rise to be as
high as the parson himself. Consequently our
hero was a universal favourite in Bluemere.
The dogs naturally adored him, because he
was their veterinary surgeon, as well as
their friend, and the little children followed
suit—for the love of babies and animals cannot be separated. The old men and women
regarded him almost as a son; the married
couples made him their confidant and arbi-
·trator in all their disputes; the youths
voted him the jolliest of companions, and,
as for the girls, if one or two of them in that

peaceful village of Bluemere had gone a step too far, and raised their hopes to a vested partnership in Briarwood House, and if their parson knew it, and felt a little flattered by their preference, what matter? He was but a man, as he said himself, and a young man after all, and the blood of youth runs as hotly in the veins of a parson as in those of an officer in the dragoons. The absurdity is, to suppose, that, by forcing a man into a particular profession, you can change his nature, and, with impunity, refuse him those licences which the world freely allows to another, and the consequence of which is, that the majority of our English parsons—let those deny the assertion who can disprove it—who have adopted the church, just as soldiers adopt the army, for a living, are only so many more proofs of the power the world's opinion has to turn a man, otherwise honourable, into a · living lie.

Bernard's mind was occupied with some

such thoughts, wondering what there existed in himself, different from other men, that he should have been elected to walk as a shining light amongst them, when his attention was arrested by the mention of his own name.

'Mr Freshfield,' called a voice as he passed by, 'I wish you would come in and speak to me for a few minutes. I tried so hard to catch you after service last Sunday, but you were too quick for me. It seems an age since you gave me a call.'

Bernard turned at once, and, with his usual courtesy, greeted a tall, angular, prim-looking old lady, who, with a shawl pinned round her head, was talking to him over a low hedge of French laurels. It was the same who had told his mother that the life he led was an example to all young men.

'Certainly, Mrs Pinner, I will come in if it will give you any pleasure. No, don't let my dogs through the gate. They will make havoc in your pretty little garden, and they are used to wait for me outside.

Is there anything that I can do for you?'
he continued, as he followed her into a
sitting-room on the ground floor.

'Oh! I have a thousand things to consult
you about relating to the parish, Mr Freshfield, but of course this is not the time. It
is past five o'clock, and you must be going
home to your dinner.'

'Never mind my dinner if you require my
services,' he replied good-naturedly.

'Now that is so like you, Mr Freshfield,
never thinking of yourself—but, no! I will
not be so selfish—what I chiefly wanted to
ask you was, if you could spare us any evening this week for just a muffin and a cup
of tea, you know, and a little quiet conversation. It would be such a privilege—and
I am particularly desirous to introduce you
to my niece.'

Now, if there was one phase of parish
life which poor Bernard particularly detested above another, it was the muffin and
cup of tea Mrs Pinner alluded to, which

generally took him away from his late dinner, and entirely deprived him of the postprandial pipe. But it was one of the little mortifications to which he made it a rule to subject himself, holding the opinion that no man is fit to guide others who is not master of his own appetites, and that to give up our inclinations for the sake of our fellow-creatures is one of the highest phases of love. So he answered readily, if not cheerfully,—

'I will accept your hospitality with pleasure, Mrs Pinner—if you cannot transact business with me as well in the morning. But I was not aware you had a niece—'

'Well, she is not a niece, Mr Freshfield. I was wrong to call her so—she is a sort of cousin on the mother's side, and very distantly connected; but she has been lately left an orphan, poor thing, so I asked her to stay with me for a few months, though I'm afraid she will be obliged to earn her own living when they are ended. But I think I can trace a providence in her coming to me. She has been very carelessly brought up, and it would be a blessed thing, wouldn't it, Mr Freshfield, if we could guide her feet into the right way before she left us again ?'

\ Bernard, who hated all cant, took no notice of Mrs Pinner's pious hope.

' Is your cousin young ?'

' Yes. Quite a girl ; but with the strangest ideas. She does not seem as if she could make enough of the country, and would idle all her time away if I allowed it.'

' Let her idle it away, Mrs Pinner. I daresay her heart is sore from her late losses. This beautiful country in this beautiful weather will speak surer peace to her than we could do in any amount of words.'

' But it seems so sinful to me, Mr Freshfield, to see a strong, hearty girl doing nothing day after day, when there is more parish work than there are hands to do it with.'

'Do you think so? I think Bluemere is admirably looked after. Sometimes I say *too* well looked after, particularly when I find that Miss Warren has counter-manded half the orders that I have given for the relief of my parishioners.'

'Ah, Miss Warren; but see how she works, Mr Freshfield, and what a head she has got. I always call her your right hand. And then she is so devoted to your interests, and she is afraid the old people impose on your good nature and get more relief from you than they really require. I am sure Miss Warren is quite an example — I often say so, and would make a model clergyman's wife.'

'She'd better go to the next parish, then,' remarked Bernard curtly. 'I know the new rector who has just been appointed there is a bachelor.'

'Oh, Mr Freshfield, you are always full of your fun; but you know that Blue-mere would be quite lost without Miss

Warren. And she was kind enough to offer to introduce Miss Moss to the Sunday school, but I am sorry to say she refused.'

' Is Miss Moss your cousin ?'

' Yes. And it's such things I want you to talk to her about, Mr Freshfield, for her notions of religion quite shock me. Only think — she wouldn't go to church with me last Sunday, but sat all day in the garden reading some frivolous story. I was ashamed that my servant should see such a thing. And she doesn't seem to have any more knowledge of the Scriptures than a heathen.'

' And do you think no one can be religious without knowing the Scriptures, Mrs Pinner ?'

' Well, of course, I know there are some who have been taught as it were of heaven itself ; but Phyllida appears to be as ignorant as a baby.'

' Well, I must come and make the acquaintance of your fair barbarian ; but please don't present me to her in the guise of a schoolmaster, or we shall make no way at all. Let me talk to Miss Moss after my own fashion, and I daresay we shall come to an understanding by-and-by.'

'I am sure you are only too good to take the trouble, Mr Freshfield. Shall we say Thursday for our little cup of tea ? And I don't think I'll tell Phyllida that you're coming, for she seems to dislike the sight of strangers so, that, ten to one, she may run out of the house just to spite me.'

'You seem to have got a bargain on your hands,' said Bernard, laughing, as he rose to take his leave. 'I suppose, as I do not see her, that Miss Moss is not indoors at present.'

'No, she disappeared after our early dinner in her strange fashion, and I haven't set eyes on her since. I'm sure it's very good of you to promise to come to us, Mr Fresh-field, and we shall look forward to it with pleasure. Quite alone, you know—a muffin and a cup of tea—next Thursday at seven —thank you so much.'

And with Mrs Pinner's murmured sentences pursuing him like buzzing flies, Bernard passed down the garden path, and, whistling to his dogs, took his way to Briarwood. He had intended to make two or three calls on the road ; but as he looked at his watch he was surprised to see how long Mrs Pinner's conversation had detained him, and determined to take a short cut home by the fields instead. His house of Briarwood was built upon a hill, and the land surrounding it was his own property. Bernard cleared a high fence, and making his way through some low brushwood which he was keeping as a pheasant preserve, entered a grove of larches which formed a foreground to his residence. He was pacing the narrow path with his eyes downcast and his thoughts far away, when he was startled by hearing a low cry of fear, followed by

a hurried exclamation. Bernard looked up.
His three dogs were leaping violently, and,
as it would seem, with murderous intent,
against the slight figure of a girl, dressed in
black, who held something to her breast with
one hand, whilst with the other she attempted to ward off the boisterous attacks
of the excited animals. Bernard whistled to
them, and then finding they did not in-
stantly obey him, he sprang forward and
belaboured them well with the stout stick
he carried in his hand. But here the girl
interposed to save her assailants from further
punishment.

'Oh, don't beat them—don't beat them!'
she cried. 'They didn't mean to hurt *me*,
the beautiful creatures, only I was so afraid
they would kill my little kitten.' And she
displayed to him a fluffy white and tabby
creature with pale blue eyes, of a few weeks
old, who was still spitting. and scratching
with all its puny might, and clinging to the
sleeve of her dress.

'Go to heel!' exclaimed Bernard in a voice of thunder to his conscience-stricken hounds, who slunk behind him, and then he took off his hat to the stranger, and trusted that her favourite was not hurt.

'Oh no, they didn't touch her; I was only afraid they would. Poor things,' she said pityingly, 'how unhappy they look! Do pat them and speak kindly to them again.'

'I had better not,' replied Bernard. 'At all events until the temptation to transgress is out of their reach. They are apt to presume upon indulgence. You love animals I see,' he added with a smile; for he loved them so well himself he felt affinity with all who shared his tastes.

'Very much—particularly dogs! they are so faithful and affectionate. I like them ever so much better than I do men and women.'

Bernard laughed.

'You think me foolish, perhaps, or wrong,

as Mrs Pinner does,—she says it is sinful
to waste time and food on animals when
there are so many poor people starving and
in want of help.'

'If we neglected our fellow-creatures to
lavish time and substance upon animals,
I should feel inclined to agree with Mrs
Pinner; but it may not lie within the range
of our duties to attend to poor people, and
these dumb creatures are certainly confided
to our care. It would be wicked to neglect
them. But from what you say, I presume
I have the pleasure of speaking to Mrs
Pinner's niece.'

'Yes; I am Phyllida Moss. And do
you, then, know my cousin Pinner?'

'Very well, indeed!'

'I am glad of that. Then perhaps she
will not think it wrong of me to have
spoken to you—cousin Pinner thinks everything wrong. She says she is going to
bring the clergyman of the parish to talk
to me about my doings.'

'Indeed! Have you been very naughty, then?'

'I can't say. I didn't go to church last Sunday—that is what bothered her.'

'Don't you like going to church?'

'Not much; it's all so prim and stiff, and the sermons make me sleepy. I like going out by myself on the hill-side and sitting on the grass and thinking better. I put my head right down in the grass and no one knows, who doesn't do that, what wonderful sights and sounds there are to be heard and seen there. The wee wee flowers, no bigger than a pin's head, like little red and blue stars with golden eyes that grow down amongst the blades; and then the insects that talk to one another, and carry their food about and build their snug houses, for all the world as well as if they were giants. And I think you know that to lie and listen to all this and think about it, and how it came to pass, does one more good than sitting for two hours within four walls and hearing a lot of things you don't care about.'

'And so do I, a thousand times over,' said Bernard heartily. 'And you have never seen the parson of Bluemere yet, then, Miss Moss ?'

'No, and I reckon I don't want to, either.'

'Why not ?'

'Oh, because cousin Pinner thinks so much of him ; it frightens me. You see I haven't been brought up amongst parsons myself. I am not good, it's no use denying it ; and what's more, I don't feel as if I ever should be.'

'Why should you say that? I am sure your impulses are good, even from the few words we have exchanged with one another.'

'I don't *feel* good. My life's been all trouble and misfortune, and that makes one hard. But it's nonsense for me to talk like this to a stranger !'

'I wish you wouldn't look on me as a stranger. I know Mrs Pinner so well, that it is only natural I should know you also.'

'You won't tell the parson?' she said, with an arch glance.

As Bernard Freshfield met her eyes, he thought—and truly—that he had never seen so lovely a woman before.

She was dressed exceedingly plain in a suit of deep black, but her bronze-coloured hair was tucked up in profusion under her plain straw hat, beneath the brim of which gleamed at him large, soft, long eyes of the clearest brown, which reminded Bernard somehow of the eyes of his favourite setter Rose. Her nose was straight; her chin pointed; her mouth a perfect bow; and her dark lashes lay on her cheek like a fringe of silk. It was a child-like face without being an innocent one—that is to say, it had an open confiding expression, and yet the languid eyes showed that the girl had passed through the experience of this world,

and known its sorrow. When Bernard
Freshfield came to know Phyllida Moss
more intimately, he found she was a strange
mixture of child and woman : of careless
mirth and thoughtful despondency ; but in
the moment of their first introduction, he only
thought her as she stood there conversing
as freely with him as if they had been acquainted all their lives, with the little kitten
clinging to her breast—simply charming.

And with each sentence she uttered, she
charmed him more.

Her last words almost upset his gravity,
but he managed to reply that he would
not tell the parson.

'Well, then, I think long prayers and
sighs and groans and texts, and all that
sort of thing, you know, nonsense. I
knew a man once,' with a shudder, ' oh,
the very worst man I ever knew, and when
it suited his purpose not to lie and gamble
and cheat, he used to go to prayers instead, and pretend to be pious, and it worked

with some folks, I suppose ; but it sickened me, and that's the truth, and I've never felt as though I could say a prayer since.'

'Mrs Pinner tells me you have lost your father and mother. Were they good parents to you ? '

'My mother was—an angel! and she's one now, I know. Nothing could knock that out of me.'

'Doubtless she is. And you used to tell her all your troubles, I daresay.'

The tears rushed to Phyllida's brown eyes.

'Ah, I used! God bless her! and she was never weary of listening, though she had enough of her own, poor soul !'

'And it comforted you to go to her ? '

'Of course it did. Who can comfort one like a mother ? '

'But she wouldn't have cared for your confidence if it hadn't been true, if you had pretended to be in trouble when you weren't really so !'

'Well—no—how should she ? '

'The church is like your mother, Miss Moss, and her children's prayers are their confidences. Whilst you have nothing to tell her, I say keep away, and don't insult her by a pretence of requiring her con- solations.'

There was a pause between them for a moment, and then Phyllida inquired,—

'Are you the parson?'

'I am; but don't let that fact frighten you. You see I am not very formidable.'

'Oh no; only perhaps I have said things I shouldn't.'

'Not at all. There is no good in a parson, unless you can speak your mind to him.'

'And do you think my mind is very wrong?'

'I think you have had some great trouble, and it has hardened you.'

'Oh, no, no,' commenced the girl vehe- mently, 'it has not hardened me! I love the flowers and the birds and trees more than I can tell you, and the little children and the animals, and I love to get out amongst them and try to fancy myself a child once more, and to begin life over again with them. That is what I want, sir, to begin life over again, to forget all that has gone before; to wipe it out as if it had never been, and to feel a girl again with the birds and flowers, a girl as I used to do before my mother died,' she said in a low wailing voice.

Bernard felt very paternal, he often did feel paternal when pretty girls bestowed their confidences on him.

'My poor child,' he replied, 'I understand you so well; I can sympathise with every word you have said. I too have known trouble, Miss Moss, very heavy trouble, not only from domestic loss, but from doubts and fears upon religious matters, similiar to if not identical with your own. Will you therefore try and look upon me not only as a friend, but as a fellow-searcher after truth, and help me with your confidences as I will help you, if possible, with my experience.'

'But I'm not fit to be your friend, Mr Freshfield—the friend of a parson. You don't know how careless I am. Mrs Pinner calls me a perfect heathen.'

'Child, you don't know of what you are talking. It is far more likely that the parson is not fit to be friends with you. But please speak of me by any name but that; I do not like it. I would rather the people of Bluemere thought of me only as their friend.'

'As a friend, then, sir, good evening. Kitty and I must be going homewards, or Mrs Pinner will have reason to think that we are lost.'

'Good-night, my child! Depend on it, it is not for nothing that we have been led to meet each other in this fantastic manner, and that your lips have been unsealed so freely to me. Good-night;

it will not be long before we meet again.'

And as Bernard Freshfield turned to watch the graceful figure in black descending the hill, cuddling the mewing kitten to her breast, he felt a strange exhilaration, as if a new interest had suddenly sprung up in his uneventful life.

CHAPTER III.

THE following morning Mrs Freshfield was considerably startled by
receiving a note from her son :—

'MY DEAR MOTHER,—Since you make a
point of my dining at Blue Mount to-day,
you must let me bring my friend Anderson
with me. He turned up unexpectedly at
Briarwood last night, and I cannot leave
him to spend the evening alone.—Yours
affectionately,   BERNARD.'

Now, Charles Anderson was an old college
chum of Bernard's, to whom he was deeply

attached. The young men had gone rather different ways since starting in life, Anderson having become deeply imbued whilst at Oxford with High Church tendencies, which had subsequently led him to the communion of Rome. But Bernard and he had never severed a link of their early friendship in consequence, and it was one of Mrs Freshfield's grievances against her son, that he stoutly refused to relinquish any part of his intercourse with Anderson. The old lady was busy when the note arrived giving her housekeeper sets of sundry linen sheets and frilled pillow cases wherewith to furnish forth the bed-chambers of the expected visitors ; but this piece of intelligence was too dreadful to be kept to herself, and she trotted off at once to communicate it to her daughter.

'Laura!' she exclaimed, with the most helpless, hopeless look upon her countenance as she came upon that young lady copying a profane love song, 'can you conceive it possible that Bernard proposes to bring Mr Anderson to dinner here this evening ?'

'Oh, I *am* glad,' replied Laura blithely, 'Charlie Anderson is so entertaining, he'll help to take the Miss Muckheeps off our hands.'

'Laura, I am surprised to hear you speak in this manner of a person who has proved himself to be so utterly without principle. Have you forgotten that Mr Anderson is a Roman Catholic—a Papist—an Apostate ?'

'One name is enough for him at a time, isn't it mamma ? But he is Bernard's friend, you know, notwithstanding, and I cannot see what his tenets have to do with his being an amusing companion.'

'Your poor brother is sadly mistaken in keeping such a friend—it is unaccountable in one who professes to hold the pure Protestant faith as it was transmitted to us by the glorious Luther. And to bring him to my table too, and to sit down with Miss Janet Muckheep. It is an insult.'

'I am sure Bernard would much rather dine at home mamma ; you know how he hates a dinner party. If you object to Mr Anderson's presence here, why not write and tell Bernard so quietly, and let him enjoy the evening with his friend at Briarwood.'

'No, Laura, my conscience would not permit of that. Who knows with what principles this poor lost soul might not imbue your unhappy brother ? We must make the sacrifice, if it is only to keep Bernard under our own eyes.'

'Well, mamma dear, let us make it then, and say no more about it. Though I must say you do not give dear Bernard credit for much steadfastness of purpose or knowledge of his own mind.'

'My dear, I know human nature better than you do, and I grieve to say that some of your brother's doctrines are anything but orthodox. However, we must make the best of this annoyance, and trust it may be overruled for good.' By which Mrs Freshfield meant that she trusted her conversation and that of Miss Muckheep might have some influence in causing the unhappy Mr Anderson to see the error of his ways. She loved to throw a stone at all Popery and Papists, and this Papist in particular,—having made of himself as it were a fearful example almost within their gates —but she had had no intention from the beginning of being deprived in consequence of the glory of seeing her son at the head of her table. So she resigned her herself, though not without many Protestant groans, to the inevitable, only hoping that Miss Janet Muckheep might not discover the principles of her fellow guest. The expected visitors arrived in the course of the afternoon, and were received by Mrs Freshfield much after the same fashion as that in which Abraham entertained the two angels. Indeed, if her real mind with regard to Miss Janet Muckheep could have

been laid bare, it would have been seen
that Mrs Freshfield did regard her as very
little lower than the angelic host. She was
not a woman of strong mind or fixed principles, notwithstanding her stock of plati-
tudes, and the old Scotchwoman's eternal
cant and dragging in of holy names and
holy subjects in every-day conversation, was
accepted by her as the very quintessence
of godliness.

Miss Janet Muckheep was the sister of
a man who was styled (or styled himself)
the Laird o' Muckheep, or *The* Muckheep,
and Miss Bella was his daughter and her
niece. The laird had married early in life,
and lost his wife within two years of the
marriage, since which bereavement he had
spent most of his time abroad. He had left
his infant daughter at Barrick-gallagas Castle,
as his feudal domains were grandly termed,
under the charge of his maiden sister, and
had only visited Scotland at intervals since.
Miss Janet affirmed that the laird's feelings

would not permit him to live on the spot where he had buried his wife; but less partial judges were not surprised that he should find pleasanter habitations than the bleak tumble-down castle of Barrick-gallagas on its stony barren lands, and more cheerful society than that of Miss Janet and Miss Bella Muckheep. There, for five-and-twenty years, therefore, had they lived together, until the younger lady had developed into a full-grown woman, and the aunt had drilled her into what she considered a perfect model of lady-like deportment and religious training. But at five-and-twenty Miss Bella was still considered and treated by her aunt as though she were a child, and scarcely permitted to eat or drink, to walk, or talk, without an injunction or a caution from her duenna.

Miss Janet herself, now an old lady of sixty, was the picture of a strong, active, hard-featured Scotchwoman. She talked such broad Scotch that it was difficult at times to understand what she said, but she professed to scorn to use the southern tongue as though it would be a disgrace to her, and she forbade her niece to do so either. She was unpleasantly candid and outspoken, never taking heed to any one's feelings, and her religious doctrine was as hard and uncompromising as her features. Yet with all Miss Janet's cant and professions of Christian humility, she had, like her friend Mrs Freshfield, one great weakness, and that was for the family blood. She could never say enough on the subject of the Muckheeps and the feudal homage paid to them in their native country as lords of the soil. To hear Miss Janet talk of Barrick-gallagas Castle and its surroundings, one would have imagined that she and her niece lived there in pomp and luxury like two queens, surrounded by their vassals. And one would have been rather surprised, if led by chance to visit this remnant of an age of princes, to find the two queens supping on oatmeal porridge, and waited on by a red-haired serving-maid without shoes or stockings, whilst the wind whistled through the ruined walls of their castle, and the thistles grew up to the tumble-down front door.

But Miss Janet did not consider she was telling or acting a falsehood by thus upholding the glory of the Muckheeps, and Mrs Freshfield listening to her grand accounts, felt her own blood quicken at the thoughts of how her Bernard's wealth entitled him to seek a match with this impoverished daughter of a long line of Scottish kings, and tried to hit upon the best plan of introducing the matrimonial alliance to his consideration. And to her intense satisfaction Miss Muckheep's own conversation seemed to land in the same direction.

''Deed!' exclaimed the old Scotchwoman, as she peered like a witch over her spectacles, ' it's weel you and I have met for a crack this simmer, Mrs Fraichfield, for the

laird himsel' talks of retairning to Barrack-
gallagas in the fa' of the yair, and ance he
sets his fut on Scottish ground it's little
they'll let him or me lose sight of the
cairs-tle again.'

'Your brother is coming home, Miss
Janet? You don't mean to say so? What
a delightful meeting is in store for you!
How you must be looking forward to his
return!'

'Ay. I don't say but we regaird it with
as much pleeasure as is ret for puir sinfu'
creatures to look fairward to that which
may never come to pairse. But it is noo
five yairs sin' the laird has seen the lassie
theer, and I'm thinkin' he consee-ders it
time he should come hame and give her
a tocher and a laird for hersel'. Bella—
heid!'

Which last mysterious sentence was not
as English ears might have interpreted a
caution only, but a straightforward direction to Miss Bella to hold up her head

—that young lady being in the habit of
stooping. Indeed, to judge from Miss
Janet's constant animadversions on her
deportment, it would be difficult to say
what portion of her niece's somewhat re-
dundant frame she did not misuse in the
using. Bella, a stout, full-faced, red-haired
young woman with blue eyes, high cheek-
bones, and the colour of a peony, jerked
up her head, as a horse does when touched
on the curb, gave a kind of snort, and went
on with her work composedly. She had
been used to these admonitions since her
infancy, and never dreamed of resenting
them at five-and-twenty.

'Oh, indeed! yes,' replied Mrs Freshfield sympathisingly; 'and I wonder that
Miss Bella has not found a husband for
herself before now. I am sure it must be
her own fault that she is still single, sweet
girl!'

'Ech, woman!' returned Miss Janet, 'but
that's noo the way the lairds o' Muckheep

marry their dairghters. I've brought up the lassie in the fear o' the Laird, and free from a' cairnal procleevities, and she kens too weel what is due to hersel', as a dairghter of *the* Muckheep, to cairst sheep's eyes at any carl that her faither hasna' chosen for her. Bella—back !'

Bella drew in the offending member with a suddenness that threw all the rest of her body out of gear ; but Miss Janet did not seem to notice the awkwardness of her appearance, although poor Laura choked with laughter, and was sternly frowned down by Mrs Freshfield.

' I am sure you need not remind me, dear Miss Janet, of how admirably you have trained your interesting charge, and the excellent principles with which you have imbued her. Any one could see from merely looking at your dear Bella how sweetly Christian humility blends with the knowledge of her ancient lineage in being descended from those grand old Scottish kings!'

'Ay, but we're a' that!' replied the old Scotchwoman with pride. 'My brither himsel' would ha' sat upon the throne o' Scotland if the country had had its reets. The Muckheeps came in a de-reect line from the fairst James, and the bluid has been untainted on their side till noo. But I'm no sayin' we can expeect the same to laist for ever; and if the lassie there can find a gude mon, and a God-fearing ane, to cheerish her innocence and keep her from cairnal procleevities in a proper fashion for ane wha has Scottish royal bluid runnin' in her veins, why, the laird and mysel' would give her our blessing with that of heaven. Bella—shoulders!'

Laura was too much interested in the conversation this time to care whether Bella carried her shoulders up to her ears or down to her heels. She was a sharp girl, and soon perceived, notwithstanding the fencing with which they carried it on, that her mother and Miss Muckheep had the same notion in their minds—namely, that her brother Bernard would make a very good match for the young lady in question, and she shuddered at the mere anticipation of such a sister-in-law.

'Ah! you must look out for a good *son*, dear Miss Muckheep,' sighed Mrs Freshfield, 'and then he is sure to make a good husband—such a son now as my Bernard has been to me. You can scarcely credit how good he is—the residents of Bluemere say they never saw such another young man— with such principles—and such charity— and such unselfishness. He is quite a father to his people, though so young. I trust he may some day marry again, for he must feel very lonely in that fine place, Briarwood, with no lady to look after it. Such furniture, Miss Janet, it seems a sin it should not be used, and his income, too, a clear two thousand a-year besides his stipend. What is a young man to do with so much money all by himself? But, as he was saying to me only yesterday, he cannot find the woman he could love in Bluemere. For my dear son is very particular, and he will marry no one who has not received a strictly religious training of the good old-fashioned sort, or who is not of undoubted birth and breeding. "Above all things, mother," he said, "she must have good blood, and be a confirmed Christian."'

Here Laura, who had been listening in silent amazement to this extraordinary com bination of requirements in a wife, broke in with her usual vehemence.

'Why, mamma, we have always considered Bernard such a radical. I didn't think he cared a pin about blue blood. I have heard him say he would take a wife off a dung-hill if he found a true wife there. And I am sure poor Alice was not very aristocratic. Her grandfather was a cotton-spinner.'

'My dear Laura,' interposed Mrs Fresh-field, 'pray do not bring in the name of that dear saint in heaven. Whatever she may

have been is no concern of ours now. And
as to your dear brother's principles, they
are strictly conservative in every way, and
the Queen has no more loyal subject than
himself.'

Miss Muckheep, whose mouth had been
watering at the description of Briarwood,
and the fortune that maintained it, took up
the cue at loyalty.

' Ay, but it's a fine thing is loyalty, Mrs
Fraichfield, and ye would say so if ye could
see the respeect and the hoo-mage that is
ay peed to the lairds o' Muckheep when
they stan' on their ain heather. King
James himsel' cou'dna have received mair
dairference fra the vassals of his coort. And
the same dairference wad be peed to a' his
de-scendants in the dereect line. And though
the bawbees air unco' guid things in them-
sels, and I wadna be sayin' that the laird
wad refuse the han' of his dairghter to any
mon wha had the siller to keep her as would
be expectit, yet I ken weel that sae lang

as he had no cairnail pro-cleevities, he
wad geeve the prair-feirence to ane wha
held con-sairvative views. Bella—chin !'

Bernard Freshfield and his friend Anderson walked over to Blue Mount some little
time before dinner, and Laura, alarmed at
the conspiracy which she had detected, took
an early opportunity to draw her brother on
one side and confide her suspicions to him.

' Bernard, dear,' she exclaimed, as she
followed him into the hall, where he went
to deposit his hat and stick, ' isn't Bella
Muckheep horrid ? *Do* say you think so.'

' She is not charming, my dear Laura,
either in person or manner, at all events,
on a first acquaintance. But what is the
matter ? Why do you look at me in that
extraordinary way ?'

' Because—I know you will not believe
me—but I assure you 'tis the truth—mamma
and Miss Janet want you to marry her.
They have been giving broad hints to each
other on the subject the whole afternoon.'

Bernard burst out laughing.

'And you are afraid your innocent brother will be entrapped into matrimony against his will, like the forlorn heroine of the last romance you indulged in, and led like a victim to the hymeneal altar, eh ?'

But Laura did not laugh. She blushed.

'Not quite that, Bernie, only—don't be angry, dear—you remember how mamma persuaded and cajoled and coaxed you before about poor Alice, until there seemed nothing for you to do but to give in. You are so good to mamma, Bernie, and so mindful of her feelings, that you forget to consider your own.'

Bernard drew his sister into the morning-room, where they could talk with greater freedom, and when he got her there he took her in his arms and kissed her.

'Thanks, dearest Laura, for your thought and care of me. But don't be afraid, little sister. Your big blundering brother will not make a second mistake. My eyes have been opened, Laura. I see and know now what love is, and I will never accept respect nor friendship nor liking instead of it. It must come to me like a revelation from heaven,—full, free, and without reserve,— pouring upon me because it has no power to contain itself, and glorified by passion as the sun tips the clouds with gold and azure. No more half hearts nor modified affections, Laura. My next love must give me all or nothing, and receive the same from me.'

'Oh, Bernie, I am so glad to hear you speak like that. It is just my own idea of what a love that terminates in marriage should be. But I dare not say so before mamma, because she calls me bold and un- maidenly to hold such opinions, and I would rather be thought anything than that. She says that if I esteem the man I marry, it is all I ought to do before I am his wife.'

'A false principle, Laura, and one that may lead to any amount of unhappiness. Love comes from God, and marriage was ordained by Him, and the man who separates the two, who marries for convenience' or conscience' sake, or because he considers it advisable, commits a blasphemy against the God of Love, and deserves all he may suffer in consequence. I would rather marry a bad woman who loved me than a good woman who did not. Love might reform the first, but mere goodness could never make me love the other. Don't mistake esteem for love, dear. They are not the same thing, and they never will be.'

'And you are quite, *quite* sure, then, that you could never come to love Bella Muckheep?'

'Quite, *quite* sure, little sister. I am afraid that I am too fond of beauty ever to be able to enjoy an ugly wife. I like to be surrounded by beautiful things—to let my eyes dwell on them—to drink in each

detail of their perfections. You know how
I value my beautiful china, my pictures
and statuettes. They are a never-failing
source of pleasure to me. My wife must
be the same. She must be lovely and
lovable, or I will die as I am. Miss
Bella's fat cheeks and unmeaning features
will never tempt your brother to alter his
condition. So you may take me back to
her presence with the most perfect safety!'

When they re-entered the drawing-room,
Miss Janet was holding forth to Mr Anderson on the perfections of her favourite
minister.

'Ech, mon!' she said, 'but ye should set
oonder the Rairverend Doctor Felinus, if
ye would hae pure darctrine and the most
eestimable example. Ay! but to hair him
cairse the sinner, and depeect the tairrors
of hell prepared for the licht-minded and
ungardly, wud mak each hair on your heed
stan' on eend. He is a rare fine preacher
is the Rairverend Doctor Felinus. It would

be wairth your wheele to traivel to Barrick-gallagas, jest to get a waird of exhoortation fra' the leeps of sae gardly a mon.'

'But my friend Mr Anderson does not belong to the same church as Dr Felinus, Miss Muckheep,' interposed Bernard at this juncture, 'added to which he has dozens of celebrated preachers of his own faith to whom he could listen with greater benefit to himself.'

'Ay, but I canna believe it,' replied Miss Janet decisively. 'No young mon could do better than to leesten to the exhoortations and the prayers of sech a meenester as Doctor Felinus, while he expoonds the glorious darctrines of Calvin, the greet refairmer. of the warld.'

'Why did you not tell us of him before!' exclaimed Mrs Freshfield enthusiastically. 'I should have been so charmed, dear Miss Muckheep, to receive your estimable minister as a guest beneath my humble roof, and to have benefited by some of the precious sayings that would have dropped like honey from his lips.'

'You, mother?' said Bernard, frowning. 'What should *you* want with the teachings of a Calvinistic minister? Haven't we parsons enough in our own country to serve your need? I can understand your wishing to receive Miss Muckheep's friend at Blue Mount, *as* a friend, but not to place yourself under his ministration as a disciple. And you of all people, who (as a rule) are so especially hard upon any one who dares to think differently from yourself in religious matters.'

Bernard accompanied this last remark with a glance at Charles Anderson, which made Mrs Freshfield colour with vexation.

'My dear Bernard,' she replied testily, 'you are utterly mistaken. It is true that I cannot tolerate a wilful turning from the truth—an abandonment of the faith in which we have been reared.'

'Come, come! we have had enough of that,' interposed her son authoritatively.

'But it does not follow,' continued Mrs Freshfield, 'that I should not derive spiritual benefit from association with a saintly man like Dr Felinus, the doctrines of whose church are precisely the same as our own.'

'That shows all you know about it,' replied Bernard. 'Dr Felinus may be, and doubtless is, an excellent man, but we do not require his teachings in Bluemere.'

'Ech, sirr!' chimed in Miss Janet, 'but ye coudna speak with greater heat if the gude dochter were a bluidy Peepist, reedy to massacre ye with the sward if ye didna sweer at ance, to adhere for aye to his demooralising and darmnatory dawctrines.'

'Madam,' said Bernard, 'I must ask you to drop all theological discussion for this evening, as my friend here, Mr Anderson, is a member of the church you speak of.'

'A meember of what?' exclaimed Miss Muckheep.

'Of the Holy Roman Catholic Church,' repeated Anderson reverently.

'And therefore,' continued Bernard, 'you will see that as his faith differs as much from mine, as mine does from that of Dr Felinus, if we wish to spend a pleasant evening together, it will be wise to put our religions in our pockets, and think only of our dinner.'

'Ay, but a Peepist!' ejaculated Miss Janet, 'a real bluidy Peepist; it is awfu' to think on, and I canna say it is what I expectit in this hoose to be asked to seet doon at the table with a disciple o' the scairleet woman!'

'Indeed—indeed, dear Miss Janet, it is not *my* doing,' interposed Mrs Freshfield.

'Mother, you forget what is due to my father's name,' said Bernard sternly; but his expression quickly changed as he turned to Miss Janet. 'Come, madam, look well at my friend, and you will see he is not so formidable an antagonist after all. Turn this way, Anderson, and let us have a good view of your apostate features.'

'Ech, sirr! but I'm no sayin' that the young mon has not a gude face of his ain, mair's the peety it should fa' doon to warr-ship blocks of stone and idols. And is it true, sirr, that the meeneesters canna marry in your misguided chairch?'

'Quite true, madam,' replied Anderson, with a bow.

'Ay! but it's an awfu' thing to con-teemplate, and I sincairly weesh that the rair-verend Dr Felinus had been hair to pint oot to ye the air-rer of your ways.'

'And I am sincerely thankful he is not,' cried Bernard, laughing, 'or we should have been victimised to listen to a religious argu-ment that would have spoiled our dinner.'

'Come, Miss Muckheep,' he added, as the butler announced that the meal was ready, 'let us leave our spiritual duties alone for awhile, and attend to the wants of the inner man. I am sure you are ready for your dinner as well as myself, and when it is

over we will join in a bumper to the healths
of the Archbishop of Canterbury, the Pope
of Rome, and Dr Felinus, and feel ever so
much better Christians for the act.'

And Miss Muckheep, although dread-
fully scandalised at hearing the name of her
favourite minister linked with those of two
such reprobates as a pope and an archbishop, possessed too many 'cairnal pro-
cleevities' of her own not to relish the idea
of a good dinner, and trotted off on Bernard's arm without another word.

'Mother!' he said, over his shoulder on
their way to the dining-room, 'I have received such a nice long letter from dear old
Nelson Cole.'

'Indeed, Bernard! and what is his news?'

'Well, he wont be home yet awhile, I
am sorry to say, but as that is the consequence of his abilities being appreciated in
the new world, his friends must not grumble
at it. And he says that when he does return, his first visit shall be to Briarwood.'

As the party seated themselves at table, Charles Anderson found himself next to Laura.

'Why do you look so solemn?' she whispered to him, laughing.

'I was only thinking — that is, hoping, Miss Freshfield, that you do not share Miss Muckheep's sentiments with regard to my religion.'

'I do not share her sentiments on any subject; you may rest assured of that,' returned Laura. 'And, above all things,' she added, with a bright look that reflected itself immediately on her companion's countenance, 'I admire freedom of thought, and the courage that puts it into action.'

CHAPTER IV.

WHEN Bernard Freshfield went to his mother's house that evening, he had fully intended asking his sister Laura to accompany him to Mrs Pinner's 'tea and muffin' on the following Thursday, and make the acquaintance of Miss Phyllida Moss. But somehow — he hardly knew why—when he had any opportunity of introducing the subject, a sudden shyness seized him and he said nothing. He was vexed with himself afterwards, and determined he would write to Laura—yet he did not write. Why was it ? The passion of love could not have made this staid young man its

victim at one interview—a single sight of
that mobile face, those starry, far-seeing
eyes and that sensitive mouth could not
have thus shaken his reason in her equi-
librium ? No ; but he instinctively felt the
approach of some great change ; and when
the love of woman does come upon man
with an overwhelming force that bears down
all barriers of circumstance or policy or
difficulty before it, he has an inkling of.
what will befall him from the very beginning. The affection which is grafted
upon esteem and a knowledge of character
may last longer, but it knows none of the
bliss that is born of mutual instinctive
passion. It is the offspring of the reason
we have cultivated—not of the nature which,
however we may lower it, came as a gift
from God, and is a part of His own essence.
When spirit is destined to meet spirit in
this world, they look out of the human eyes
and tell the truth at once. So, although
Bernard Freshfield had only spoken in a

grave and somewhat catechising manner to a young girl who, without being shy or re- served, had scarcely smiled once in answer- ing him, he had an undefinable feeling at the idea of meeting her again—a desire that made him excited at the prospect, combined with a reluctance that almost in- duced him not to go at all. But it was *almost* —not quite. Something—the nineteenth century will laugh at me for calling it his fate, yet why should it not have been his fate since things happen in this world whether we will or no, and no power nor prayer of ours seems able to prevent them —something at any rate, that was stronger than his own inclination, drew him to Mrs Pinner's on Thursday evening, although he thought that he would much rather have remained at home. And when he reached his destination and found that Miss Annie Warren, decked out in white muslin and pink ribbons, was one of the guests invited to meet him, he thought so still more.

Miss Warren, as has been already inti-
mated, was a parochial light in Bluemere,
although some people were unkind enough
to say she had not found out her vocation
until there was a good-looking young parson
for her to work under. She was a dark,
Jewish-looking woman, with a profusion of
black hair which she wore in innumerable
twists, plaits and curls, and was now considerably over thirty years of age; never-
theless she cherished very strong hopes of
stepping into the vacant shoes at the
rectory. She had made herself necessary
to Bernard's late wife by taking all her
parish and domestic duties off her hands,
until the weak-minded Alice had imagined
she could not order a dinner without the
assistance of her friend. So it came to
pass that, when the poor girl fell into the
decline of which she died, Miss Warren
not only attended to the wants of the
villagers, but constituted herself Mrs Freshfield's head nurse. And the husband, how-

ever much he disliked her, could not but appear grateful for a kindness which professed to be disinterested.

But when Alice died, Bernard found himself placed in rather an awkward position with regard to Miss Warren.

She had obtained so firm a footing at Briarwood that she almost seemed a fixture there; and it was not without calling in the aid of his mother that he could persuade the young lady that her duties as nurse and housekeeper were at an end.

But as for stopping her interference in the parish, he found that to be almost an impossibility. Miss Annie Warren was always so ready to defer to his wishes and carry out his directions, that he could find no actual fault with her, and the only objection he really had to her acting as his lieutenant was, that she so identified his interests with her own, that the people of Bluemere began to believe they were similar.

She had an obnoxious habit too of speaking of '*our* dear Alice' and '*our* dear lost saint,' for which Bernard could not rebuke her, and yet which jarred upon him more with each repetition; so that he did not feel particularly pleased when Miss Warren came skipping to open Mrs Pinner's garden gate,—she had an infantine habit of skipping, 'as if she were bounding on cork soles,' which made her look terribly young,—and scolded him for being late, as if he were her own property.

'You naughty, naughty man,' she cried playfully. 'Here have we been waiting for you for the last twenty minutes. I don't know what colour the tea can be by this time, but the poor muffins are as dry as a bone. But you *sha'n't* be scolded,' she went on, as she passed her arm familiarly through his, and led him triumphantly up the garden path. 'I daresay you are tired, poor dear, with parish work, and want your tea as much as any of us. Tell me what you've been doing this afternoon. Have you visited the almshouse, and, by the way, did you go and see the man at Gray's, who broke his leg falling from the haycart?'

Bernard tried to wriggle his arm out of her's, but without effect.

'No; I haven't been to Gray's,' he answered somewhat curtly, 'nor to the alms-houses either. I was too much occupied with other things.'

'Your sermon for next Sunday, perhaps,' suggested Miss Warren. 'Well, I think it is better for you to write it early in the week. You know how tired you generally are by Saturday afternoon.'

'Excuse me,' was the young man's reply, as he stooped down to tie an imaginary shoe-string, and thus released himself from Miss Warren's hold. He was determined not to be led into the presence of Mrs Pinner and her cousin, like a sheep to the slaughter.

'Here he is,' exclaimed Miss Warren, as

she preceded him into the sitting-room ; ' and now, Mrs Pinner, you must be good enough to let him have his tea at once, and not say a word to him until he has finished it, because he is just "done up" with work and worry, and I don't know what *your* opinion may be, but I think it is awfully good of him to come here and see us at all.'

' Miss Warren gives me credit for a self-denial of which I am utterly incapable,' said Bernard, as he shook hands with Mrs Pinner and two or three other ladies, and looked anxiously round the room for a form which did not appear; 'for, in the first place, Mrs Pinner, I am as fresh as a daisy, having been asleep half the afternoon under my big mulberry tree ; and in the second, I could have no greater pleasure than in ful-filling my engagement with you.'

' Ah ! dear Mr Freshfield, everybody in Bluemere knows how good and self-deny-ing you are ; there is no need to try and hide your light under a bushel,' sighed his hostess.

'No, indeed, and he couldn't do it if he tried,' pertly interposed Miss Warren. 'Who should know that better than myself, who have seen him under the most painful circumstances. Ah! that sad, sad autumn, two years ago, when our darling lay, day after day, beneath the mulberry tree, and we never knew, from hour to hour, which would be the last. No one could have watched your behaviour *then*, Mr Fresh-field, and doubted if you were self-denying or not.'

'Well, let us talk of something more con-genial than my domestic virtues,' replied the young man hastily, as he turned his back upon Miss Warren. At that moment he positively hated her and her reminiscences, and could have boxed her ears with the greatest pleasure, had it but been consistent with his profession as a parson.

'I hope Miss Moss is well,' he continued

to Mrs Pinner, 'and that I shall have the pleasure of seeing her this evening?'

'Yes, she is well enough, thank you. She was here a minute ago, but went upstairs as you entered the gate. Miss Warren, my dear, will you call Phyllida for me?'

'Such an extraordinary girl,' whispered Miss Annie familiarly, as she passed his chair, 'it is hardly to be credited that such a creature belongs to the same race as our sweet lost Alice. I hardly know what you'll make of her! She is not *our* style by any means.'

Bernard shook his head impatiently, as though a gad-fly had buzzed past his ear as Miss Warren, with, an arch smile, left the room.

'I suppose Miss Moss has told you of our meeting in the Briarwood copse on Monday?' he said, addressing Mrs Pinner.

'No, indeed! What an odd thing that she should conceal it. Oh, Mr Freshfield, she is a very strange girl! I am almost afraid you will blame me for asking her to Bluemere. And so you have already seen her? And what was she doing at Briar-wood? Not trespassing, I sincerely hope?'

'Indeed, *no*,' replied Bernard earnestly, 'Miss Moss was only taking an ordinary walk, and I trust she will make use of my grounds whenever she feels disposed to do so. And Mrs Pinner,' he continued in a lower key, 'I don't think you should speak of your cousin in such terms before strangers. You will give them an unfavourable impression of Miss Moss. I see nothing extra-ordinary in her myself; we had a long talk together, and her ideas are much the same as other people's, except perhaps that she expresses them more openly. And pro-bably they are due to her bringing up as much as to anything else. Where did you tell me she came from?'

'She came to me straight from St Domingo, Mr Freshfield, where some of

her mother's friends reside, and I believe
you may call it her home, though she has
travelled a great deal about. My cousin,
Agnes Summers, went out to the West
Indies, where she married her first husband, and this girl is her daughter by a
second marriage. However, I never knew
either Agnes or the men she married,
so it's of little consequence to me either
way, only I hope I haven't done wrong in
letting Phyllida come to Bluemere.'

' I am *sure* you have not. Take my
word for it,' replied the parson fervently,
and Mrs Pinner believed in him so fully
that she began to think that, on the con-
tary, she had done a very clever thing.

' Here is Phyllida !' she exclaimed, a
moment after, as Miss Moss entered the
room with Annie Warren. She was still
dressed in deep black, and the lace round
her throat was the only ornament that
relieved her sombre attire. The two young
ladies in white muslin, and the widow in

purple satin who formed the other guests, exchanged furtive looks and smiles at the simplicity of the stranger's dress ; but Bernard saw only the humid eyes and the marvellous complexion, and the parted lips like rose leaves with the dew on them, as he rose and clasped the hand she extended to him. After Phyllida's entrance and the few commonplace inquiries that suceeeded it, a blight seemed to fall upon our parson as regarded conversation, and the ladies had all the chatter to themselves.

The tea and muffins duly made their appearance, and Bernard was conscious of being assiduously waited on by Miss Warren and Miss Masters and Miss Lacy, whilst Mrs Pinner and Mrs Norman talked to him in soft, purring tones, and he answered their inquiries at haphazard, and was half alive to what was passing round him. For Miss Moss was sitting at an open window at the opposite side of the room, with her face from him, and he kept watching the soft evening light as it shimmered on the rippling waves of her rust-coloured hair, and wondering to himself why each time she made a movement, as though she would turn and look at him, a shock ran through his veins as if they had been sub-jected to electricity. It was quite time our young parson was recalled to himself.

'Now, didn't I say he was regularly "done up,"' ejaculated the shrill voice of Miss Warren. 'Look at his tea and muffin, both as cold as stones. As if he could deceive *me*,' she continued in a tone of triumph, 'who have watched his moods for weeks together. Have you forgotten the time when I had regularly to *coax* you to take your breakfast, Mr Freshfield, and if I left you to yourself for a minute you'd be off and leave it untasted on the table? Ah, those were sad times, weren't they? but mingled with much sweetness, and blessed to both of us, I hope.'

'I am sure they were times that neither

you nor Mr Freshfield can ever forget,
live as long as you may,' chimed in Mrs
Pinner, 'for the whole village mourned
with you and with him. Such a life, and
such a death. Ah,—sweet saint.'

'Ah, indeed,' sighed Mrs Norman, and
all the young ladies looked mournfully
sympathetic.

'We often think of you, dear Mr Freshfield, in your lonely rooms, and pray for
you. It was as terrible loss to incur so
early in life ; but depend upon it, it was
not sent for naught. It will be overruled,
and there are happy days in store for
you still at dear Briarwood.'

'I hope so,' replied Bernard simply, and
he meant to say no more, but catching a
glance of *too* much sympathy from the black
eyes of Miss Warren, he went on hurriedly,
'I know, my good friends, that you all feel
for me, and mean it for the best, but I think
it is almost as well not to allude to such
things, at all events in company like the

present. The past *is* past, you know, and
I am a great advocate for burying the past
as much as lies in our power. I think it
was intended we should do so. I think
the Creator meant us to be as happy as
we can, consistently with an honourable
living; and that when He sends us trouble,
He does not wish us to nurse it longer
than is necessary. And, added to this, I
feel almost as if I should be exciting your
sympathy on false pretences, if I did not
tell you that, whatever I may have passed
through, I am very happy now. I can never
feel really lonely, you know, with my good
mother and sister to keep me company, and
I have no present intention nor desire to
have any other society than theirs, and
that of my friends of Bluemere. So let
us talk of something more cheerful than my
past troubles; which, I can assure you, Mrs
Pinner, have nothing to do with the present
deplorable condition of my tea and muffin.
It is a real shame of me to have neglected

them; but if the truth must be told, I dine too late to make a good hand at tea, and I came here for the pleasure of your society only. Will you forgive me, and let some of these young ladies seal my pardon with a little of their charming music?'

By which it will be seen that the Reverend Bernard Freshfield had not been able to keep himself entirely free of using the small change which passes current in village society. But whilst he caused the hearts of Miss Lacy and Miss Masters to flutter with excitement at his request, as they looked out their most pathetic ballads for his edification, Bernard's thoughts were fixed only on the silent figure by the window, which had not once joined in the general conversation. Phyllida had looked up suddenly, it is true, when Bernard said that it was a duty to bury the past, and her wonderful eyes had met his, and told him intuitively that she too had a past to bury; but the glance had lasted but a second, like a flash of lightning though—like the lightning, it revealed so much, and he longed to see the dark lashes raised again. The young ladies were warbling 'Two Wandering Stars' together by this time, whilst Miss Warren turned over the leaves of the music, for it was Miss Warren's *rôle* to appear as the benefactor, help and guide of everybody in the parish, and Mrs Pinner was enlightening Mrs Norman on the subject of Miss Moss's antecedents. So Bernard left his seat, as nervously as if he were a school-boy, and approached the window where the stranger sat alone.

'Not one word for me this evening?' he inquired in a low voice.

'Do you require any? I thought you were so fully occupied,' replied Phyllida, 'and what should *I* say in a company like this?'

'Probably something more interesting than anyone else. Mrs Pinner tells me you are a great traveller.'

The girl coloured visibly.

'She invented the information then! *I* never told her so. I *have* travelled of course —who has not in these days—but not half as much as some people.'

'But you came from the West Indies?'

'Yes, my mother had many friends there. I thought at one time I would make it my home for good! But circumstances caused me to alter my mind.'

'I am so glad of those circumstances.'

'Why?'

'Cannot you guess? If they had not happened, we might never have met.'

'That would have been no great loss to you, Mr Freshfield,' she answered quietly. 'I am not a good subject for conversion. You will only waste your time attempting it.'

He was about to answer her, when Miss Warren distracted his attention.

'Mr Freshfield, isn't it wrong of Miss Lacy's brother? He is a clergyman, you

know, in London, and he actually allows
his wife to go to the theatres.'

'Really, Miss Warren, I am no judge
of another man's actions. If Mr Lacy considers the play a suitable amusement for
his wife, he is perfectly justified in letting
her attend it.'

'But think of the scenes enacted there—
think of the dreadful characters of the poor
lost actors and actresses! I remember when
our beloved Alice—'

'Hush! please don't let us revert to that
name,' interposed Bernard; 'I am not aware
that I was ever narrow-minded enough to
attempt to bias the opinion of any one in
any matter that is not strictly forbidden.
My sister Laura is very fond of the theatre,
and I have never tried to dissuade her from
attending it.'

'But you don't go yourself, Mr Freshfield?' said Mrs Pinner.

'Because there is no theatre in Bluemere,'
he laughed, and then he added, 'that is

quite another thing. I may refrain from doing so for expediency's sake, but it does not follow that I consider it wrong. On the contrary, I wish I could indulge my very natural inclination that way. And I daresay many are of the same opinion. What do *you* say, Miss Moss? Are you not fond of the theatre?'

He had to repeat his question before she answered in a very low but decided voice,—

'*No!*'

'Perhaps you have seen too much of it, and are already *blasée*?'

She shook her head again.

'It is not that—but if *your* conscience approves of it, don't try and persuade them to like it in order to follow your opinion. It is not the theatre, Mr Freshfield, but the company and the excitement and the late hours. Oh, let them continue to love the pure air of the country and the innocence and freshness that is around them, and don't imbue them with a second-hand taste for what can never do them so much good as harm.'

She spoke rapidly, and almost in a whisper, but he could hear every word, and marked the glow which overspread her features, and bespoke the sincerity which actuated her speech.

'Thank you,' he said in answer; 'you have become my teacher.'

'No! no! I did not mean that; it would be the height of presumption—only you do not know, you cannot tell.'

'Do you sing?' he asked, to fill up the pause. 'Will you sing for us?'

'Oh yes; Phyllida can sing. She has a very pretty pipe of her own,' replied Mrs Pinner, who, with the rest, had been unable to catch the substance of what had passed between her cousin and the parson. But Miss Moss seemed unwilling to show off her accomplishments.

'*Do* sing,' urged Bernard, 'for *me*.'

' Are you fond of music ? '

' Of *music* ? Yes. But one seldom hears it.'

Phyllida went to the piano and struck the opening chords of Ascher's song, ' Alice, where art thou ? '

' You can't sing that!' cried Miss Annie Warren, in a nervous heat. Phyllida looked up to her for explanation.

' Why not ? '

' Because—it's the very name. Oh, Mrs Pinner, please make her sing something else!'

' And why are we not to hear Ascher's song ? ' demanded Bernard, who knew the ballad, and the reason Miss Warren objected to it perfectly well.

' Oh, if *you* can bear it, let her go on,' replied Miss Warren huskily ; ' but as for myself, I must ask leave to quit the room,' and with that she disappeared.

' What am I to do ? ' asked Phyllida, bewildered.

'Go on,' said the parson, and so she went on, and sang her song through to the end. When she had finished, every one except Bernard looked as grave as a judge.

'Thank you so much,' was his comment. 'I never heard anybody sing so beautifully as you do, before.'

She had sung the song in a manner most unusually heard in private life. For though she made no effort, and indeed had taken but little trouble in the matter, her voice was so well trained that she could not use it ill, and the simple song of love and death appealed to the hearts of all present.

When it was concluded, Bernard took possession of the chair by the window that she had vacated, and looked more solemn than before.

'There, you cruel girl, see what you have done!' exclaimed Miss Warren, as she re-entered the room; 'you have made him downright miserable, and no wonder.'

'But he asked for the song himself. And

why should he mind it more than any other ?' rejoined Phyllida, glancing somewhat ruefully at the parson's downcast face.

' He told you to go on because he was too polite to stop you ; but it has awakened the most sorrowful memories in his breast. His wife's name was Alice ; the sweetest creature you ever saw, and my dearest friend, and we watched by her dying bed together, and I know what he suffered, dear, dear creature ! and what an excellent husband he was to her, and more like a brother than a friend to me.'

Phyllida's lip curled.

' Perhaps you will be able to console him, then,' she said shortly as she turned away.

' Oh, Mrs Pinner, did you ever hear of such heartlessness !' exclaimed Miss Warren, as she repeated the circumstance during a whispered confidence in the corner of the room.

' It is a sad insight, my dear ; but perhaps

the poor thing has never been happy enough to know what trouble is, and will be mercifully chastened before long. But tell Mary to bring in the tray, my dear. A little refreshment may rouse our dear minister from his sad recollections.'

The little refreshment, which consisted of stale sponge cakes and bad sherry, did have the desired effect of rousing Bernard, for, in his anxiety to avoid taking any himself, he waited so assiduously on his fair friends, and talked so incessantly to them, that they did not notice the fact that he neither ate nor drank, and Miss Moss followed his example, she neither ate sponge-cakes nor drank sherry.

'I am glad to see the signs of a little feeling in your cousin,' said Miss Warren, with her mouth full, to Mrs Pinner. 'She can-not take any refreshment. She is evidently thinking over the mischief she has done.'

'Ah! these things are all ordained for us, and doubtless it will be overruled,' replied

Mrs Pinner, and she would have heaved a pious sigh, only a bit of the stale sponge-cake went the wrong way and made her cough instead.

When the ladies rose to get their cloaks and bonnets, and Bernard realised that his term of purgatory was over, he looked round for Miss Moss in vain. It was a lovely summer night, and the village was as light as though it were day, yet Mrs Pinner's guests, Miss Warren in particular, had quite depended on securing Mr Fresh-field's services to escort them to their homes. But their hopes proved futile. Mr Fresh-field shook hands with them all at the garden gate, but remained inside of it himself.

'What *can* he be stopping for?' said Miss Warren anxiously, as they were compelled to start without him.

'Perhaps he has some parish matter to speak of with Mrs Pinner,' suggested Mrs Norman.

'Nonsense,' was the sharp retort; 'as if she had anything to do with the parish! Mr Freshfield consults *me* only in such matters,—indeed, he leaves them to me to settle without any consultation. I always did the work for him in dear Alice's lifetime, and I have never relinquished it since.'

'Wont it place you in rather an awkward position if Mr Freshfield marries again?' inquired the widow, who, like all the eligible ladies of Bluemere, aspired to the post of parson's wife, and was proportionately jealous of Miss Warren's interference.

'I don't think so,' was the fair Annie's reply, delivered with a certain secret satisfaction that aggravated her rivals.

'Laura Freshfield told me she hoped her brother would marry again, and soon, too,' remarked yellow-haired Miss Lacy, 'and have another fair wife into the bargain, for she hates dark women.'

'As if Mr Freshfield would choose a wife to suit his *sister's* fancy!' ejaculated Miss

Warren, with an indignant toss of her head, which resulted in silence, and lasted until the ladies parted at their respective doors.

Meanwhile, the parson, standing in Mrs Pinner's garden, had asked that lady's permission to light a cigar, which she, from the door-step, with her head enveloped in a woollen wrap, had graciously accorded. It was a very obstinate cigar, however, and after at least a dozen *allumettes* had been struck on the heel of his boot, and gone out of themselves, whilst Bernard's eyes roved up and down the house and garden path, he spoke again,—

'I don't think I said good-night to Miss Moss, Mrs Pinner. I hope she will not think me neglectful?'

'Oh no, indeed, Mr Freshfield, but I will go and look for her, and if she has not yet retired I will send her out to you.' And the old lady, who was very glad to get out of the night air, beat a hasty retreat.

As she disappeared, a slight form came

round the other side of the house, and a subdued voice said,—

'Were you asking for me, sir?'

Bernard turned to her with alacrity. Oh, if Miss Warren could only have seen it!

'I was, indeed. I should have been sorry to return home without wishing you good-bye.'

'And I was waiting here to speak to you also, that is, if I could manage it, without the presence of all those women.'

'All those women have gone home,' laughed Bernard, 'and you may speak with impunity.'

'But it is no laughing matter, sir. I guess I have wounded your feelings to-night, and stirred up old memories which you de-sired to forget. I am very sorry for it—that is all I can say, but I did it unintentionally. I know what trouble is myself, and I would have bitten out my tongue sooner than care-lessly rake up yours.'

'But, my dear child,' replied Bernard, 'I

don't know to what you allude. You have done nothing this evening but afford me exquisite pleasure by your beautiful voice and manner of singing.'

' You grew silent afterwards, and Miss Warren accused me of cruelty in singing a song with that name in it. She said it was the name of your dead wife, whose loss you mourn so much, and I am sorry for it, since it may make you dislike me.'

Bernard's reply was slow in coming, and he prefaced it by placing his hand over the one with which she leaned on the top of the garden gate.

' I cannot speak to you openly,' he said, ' and yet I wish you to understand me. Will you believe me, Miss Moss, when I say that Miss Warren is utterly mistaken in thinking that I did not enjoy your song. And yet it made me feel sad in the midst of pleasure. Why? Because I have never yet found my " Alice ! " She is still in Shadow Land, for me and my heart is always crying "Where art thou?" You may think it very strange for a widower to speak like this, but I feel I can trust you with my secret. I have been a husband, but I have never been married. My wife—the woman who is to be *one* with me in heart and soul I—have yet to meet. And perhaps I may never meet her. Perhaps I may end my life still crying, "Where art thou?" And that is what made me sad—not your sweet song, and sweeter voice.'

'Poor girl,' sighed Phyllida, with a sort of gasping sob.

'To whom do you allude?'

'To your dead wife.'

'No, don't say that. Don't run away with the idea that because I had a want unsatisfied, she must needs have been unhappy. I thank God I sincerely believe she led as peaceful and contented a life as is possible. and died without the faintest idea but that I had done the same. She was a good, dear girl, and I was fond of her, and grateful to her for all her forbearance with me, but I was not happy with her—that is all.'

'Well, and I repeat my words,' said Phyllida, ' " Poor girl ! " doubly poor in having failed to come up to the requirements of the lofty position to which you raised her.'

' The "lofty position " of a parson's wife,' laughed Bernard. ' It is evident you are not imbued with English ideas, Miss Moss, or you would not have made such a terrible mistake. We don't think much of parsons in England—and as for the parsons' wives, they are nowhere.'

' But isn't it a great thing to be the wife of a *real* good man,' said the girl thoughtfully ; ' to be his companion and his friend, and to learn to be as good yourself as he is ? '

' It is a better thing to be his all on earth,' replied this material young man earnestly. ' I am afraid too many women accept men as husbands on the score of

their supposed goodness, and find afterwards
that a sense of duty alone supplies a very
unexhilarating sort of wine with which to
fill the cup of life.   Parsons' wives, as well
as the wives of other men, Miss Moss, must
build their married happiness on love—on
true and mutual love—or expect it to fail
them in their most urgent need.'

'I should think that to be the wife of a
good man was sufficient happiness for any
woman on earth.   Think what it is—I mean
only fancy what it must be—to be tied to
a bad man, a thief or a murderer' (with a
shudder), 'always swearing at you or cursing
you—and then see what a heaven the other
would look like.'

'But you are imagining an extreme case,
Miss Moss, such an one as could never
enter except into your imagination.   How
you tremble.   Do you feel the night cold?'

'No, no!' the girl replied with a
shaking voice, that sounded ominously like
tears.

' 'You are sad,' said Bernard kindly. 'You are in trouble. What is it?'

But all the answer Phyllida gave was to throw her hands up to her face and give vent to a sudden burst of grief.

'Oh, how I wish I was dead!' she exclaimed as she dashed the tears from her eyes with an impatient gesture at her own weakness; 'how I wish I was at rest with your Alice or the thousand other girls that have dropped to sleep in this peaceful village before care or misery came upon them.'

'Don't say that,' cried Bernard, startled out of all propriety by her unexpected emotion. 'If you only knew what I feel, what it would be to me,' and then, recalling himself just in time, he added more calmly, 'Miss Moss—Phyllida, if I may call you so— never do such a thing again as to wish for death, however tempted you may be. It is foolish and wrong. Death is not oblivion, remember, and whatever ills we have to bear in this life, may be doubled in the world to come. I guess—I feel that you have suffered : be patient, look on me as your friend, and some day you may gather heart to come and tell me all, and I will give you absolution for it.'

'Oh no—not you—not *you!*' exclaimed the girl fearfully. ' I could not tell *you.*'

'Then I will be your friend without re-ceiving your confidence. Any way, I must —I *will* be—your friend.'

The soft brown eyes went up to meet the glance of his, and sunk beneath it. Bernard pressed the hand he had again taken in his own.

'Phyllida,' he whispered; and then he heaved a sigh and turned on his heel and walked slowly down the lane.

She stood for a minute where he had left her, gazing after him.

'Oh, what is this?' she asked herself with a sort of fearful joy.

'Phyllida,' said the shrill voice of Mrs

Pinner, 'have you said good-night to the minister?'

'Yes, cousin. I have said good-night to him,' replied the girl as she returned to the house.

CHAPTER V.

IT is the teaching of the world that has made us lay down the axiom that to act upon impulse is a folly. How few of our impulses are wrong. What benevolent impulses, and sympathetic impulses, and generous impulses we relinquish upon second thoughts, for fear that we may be 'taken in,' or 'make fools of ourselves,' or 'not show a proper pride,' and the world—the heartless, lying, snobbish world—may jeer at an impulsive error. Ah, better to be taken in a thousand times than break one heart (and that one perhaps our own) from a dilatoriness that can never be amended. Yet so strong is the influence of our childhood's teaching, that we seldom act on impulse without entertaining a host of misgivings as to whether we have not done wrong.

Bernard Freshfield felt so as he walked home that night. He had only done the most natural thing for a young and impressionable man to do, when brought in contact with a young woman in trouble. He had tried to console her, and he had permitted his voice and his eyes to convey the sympathy he felt. If he had followed his impulses to their full extent, he would have kissed the sweet, tearful face that was uplifted to his in the moonlight, but at this point he had restrained himself. Yet he blamed his own weakness as he walked home to Briarwood, and condemned his conduct as unbecoming his profession, and wished he had not said 'Phyllida,' in that particularly soft

and winning voice as he left her side, or
that he was at liberty to act and feel
like other men of his age and position.

He vexed himself on every point, in fact,
until he reached his destination, and made
grand resolutions to be more circumspect for
the future. What should a minister of the
gospel, he thought, have to do with falling
in love at first sight? It was indecorous
and unseemly! Besides, it couldn't *be* love,
ablaze in this manner at a moment's notice,
and for a woman he knew nothing of, and
had never seen but once before. It
must be some baser passion, born only of
a beautiful face and lustrous languid eyes,
and it was his duty to trample it under
foot as a temptation of the devil.

He went to bed in this praiseworthy
frame of mind, and he waked in the morning with but one idea in his head—how
could he contrive to meet Phyllida Moss
again! He wanted to bring her to Briarwood—to see her walk through his rooms

and sit in his chairs, and leave the influence of her enchanted presence behind her
when she left again. A happy thought
struck him! The Miss Muckheeps' visit
to Bluemere as his mother's guests, rendered
it almost imperative on him to show them
some attention at Briarwood. He would
invite the whole party over to meet Mrs
Pinner and her cousin, and one or two
other friends. They would not have a
formal dinner only, they should spend a
day there—a whole, long, sunny, happy,
heavenly day amongst the flower gardens
and shrubberies of Briarwood. As soon as
Bernard had conceived this idea, there was
no longer any rest for him until he had
put it into execution. He sprung from
his bed, and walked over to Blue Mount,
delighting his mother by appearing at the
breakfast-table in the most affable humour
with her and everybody else.

'We have had such a glorious summer,
and the country is looking so beautiful,

that it really is a sin for anyone to remain in bed when he may be abroad with nature,' he said, in excuse for his early visit. 'My old gardener, Armstrong, has turned Briarwood into a perfect Paradise. I hope you are going to bring your visitors over to see my flowers, mother? Are you fond of a garden, Miss Muckheep?' he added to Miss Janet.

'Ay,' replied the old woman in one long drawn-out syllable. 'I'm no denyin' that the flo-ors air as bonnie as the reest o' the wairks o' the creation, but to be ower fond of a gair-den or a doog, or a beestie of any sairt is a cair-nal procleevity fra which I thank the Laird I ha' been presairved. Bella—een!'

'Ah, well,' replied Bernard, laughing; 'perhaps I should have said are you an admirer of nature instead, Miss Janet? Any way, if you and your niece will honour me by accompanying my mother and sister to Briarwood some day, I think I can show you as pretty a flower-garden, on a small scale, as is to be found in the county.'

Mrs Freshfield became quite excited at this proof of her son's evident desire to make himself agreeable to her friends.

' I am sure you will enjoy it, dear Miss Janet,' she interposed. ' My Bernard is an excellent host, and Briarwood itself is worthy of a visit. I want you to see the rooms and the furniture,' she continued, in a lower and more confidential key. ' *Such* a drawing-room, all ebonised chairs and tables, with pale pink hangings, and the library, too, in solid oak and morocco leather. No expense was spared, I can assure you, in fitting it up, for I felt I could not do too much for the wife of my beloved son, as I shall feel again, if the happy day ever arrives for me to welcome a new mistress to Briarwood.'

' Eh, weel, woman, it's na' seelks nor sai-tins as ye maun set your mind upon, but a clean hairt and a reet speerit, and

then a' the reest maun follow in due coorse.
Not that I wudna be sayin' that a guid
tocher is an eestimable thing to set up the
hoose with, and I trawst that Bella's carle
will be fain to geeve her foorniture accair-
din' to her station ; but we mauna think
too much of oor sinful bodies and the
cawm-forts of this wairld.'

'No, no ; of course not,' replied Mrs
Freshfield, who was rather taken aback
by this unexpected rebuke, 'still I am
sure you will say you never saw anything
more elegant than the decorations of
Briarwood.'

Bernard, meanwhile, had drawn his
sister aside.

'I want you to write two or three invitations for me, Laura. They will come
better from mother than from myself.'

'Why, Bernard, are you going to have a
party ?'

'Oh no; nothing particular. Only a
few friends will make the visit more agree-

able to the Muckheeps, and it is a good opportunity for me to pay off some old debts in that way.'

' To whom shall I write, then ? '

' To the Ashleighs. Ask Captain and Mrs Ashleigh, and their son. I have dined there several times this year.'

'Very good ; and who else ? '

' The Langleys ; they are nice girls, and have two officers staying with them. And, let me see! You may as well ask Mrs Pinner and her cousin, Miss Moss.'

' Has Mrs Pinner a cousin ? ' asked Laura in surprise. ' When did she come ? I never heard of her.'

' I thought the village crier—Miss Warren —would have been sure to tell you all about her. Miss Moss has been in Bluemere for some weeks, and I have met her at the Pinners.'

' And is she nice, Bernie ? '

' Oh, she's well enough ; a little barbarian, fresh caught from St Domingo, but with

more in her perhaps than the generality
of her sex—(no offence meant, my dear,
and I hope none " took ").'

' Never mind, I am used to your com-
pliments. But is it necessary to ask this
girl, Bernie ? You can't have everybody.'

' She may as well come,' replied her
brother indifferently, ' Mrs Pinner will not
care to walk backwards and forwards to
Briarwood alone.'

' Very well. Any more ? '

' No ; the others will be men, and I will
write to them myself. '

' Not Miss Warren ? '

' Certainly not Miss Warren, she is detestable ! ' replied Bernard, with unnecessary
warmth.

' Oh dear ! ' laughed Laura with a mis-
chievous look. She was well aware of
Annie Warren's aspirations with regard to
Briarwood and its master, and was not sorry
to think that for once that individual would

be unable to boast of her intimacy with the family of Freshfield.

Bernard remained at Blue Mount all the morning, and it was arranged that the festivities of Briarwood were to take place on the following Tuesday, and to consist of a collation on the lawn at five o'clock, and a supper in the house at half-past nine. Croquet, lawn-tennis, and archery were to be the amusements of the afternoon, and the parson was actually rash enough to pro-pose a fiddler and a dance on the green, to give them an appetite for supper, but Miss Janet nipped his frolicsome propensities in the bud.

' If ye will ha' seckit cairnal pairstimes at yon hoose of Bree-arwud, never expectit to see me within its wairls, Mr Fraichfield. You mak me bloosh to hear ye coonten-ance sic ungawdly plee-sures. Na, na ; Bella doesna' set fut in Bree-arwud till ye can tell me there will be na sic profane seeghts to meet her ee'. Bella—shoolders !

'Oh, no, no! dear Miss Janet, Bernard was only joking. Were you not, my son?' exclaimed Mrs Freshfield, horrified at the turn things were taking in her visitor's mind. 'He would never *dream* of anything so frivolous as dancing. Would you, Bernard? We have all agreed long ago that it is a vain and godless amusement, and quite unfitted for one of his sacred calling.'

'Well, I don't know about *dreaming* of it, mother,' replied Bernard frankly. 'I am afraid I very often *do* dream of it, and wish it were more feasible; but I can assure you and Miss Janet that there shall be no dancing at Briarwood if the idea is the least offensive in your eyes.'

'That's my good son!' replied Mrs Freshfield, and so the matter was happily settled, and Bernard returned home to consult his housekeeper about the preparations for the coming entertainment, and to pass, as best he might, the few hours of feverish

suspense which must elapse before he received an answer from Mrs Pinner.

It came at last, and it was favourable.
It would give Miss Moss and herself the
greatest pleasure to accept the Reverend Mr
Freshfield's kind invitation for Tuesday next.

What else did he expect the woman to
say, considering that all days were dis-
engaged days in Bluemere, and an invitation
to Briarwood or Blue Mount was considered
the very height of honourable dissipation.
Of course everybody said that they would
come, and only too glad to do so.

Yet the foolish, love-stricken young man
felt the hot blood course wildly through
his veins as he read Mrs Pinner's commonplace reply, and he raised the old woman's
crabbed writing to his burning lips.

The weather behaved as it ought to do
on that particular Tuesday, and the August
sun was streaming like a flame of glory
over hill and dale and foliage and flowers, as
Bernard Freshfield stood in the portico of

Briarwood to receive his guests, dressed in a brown velveteen coat with a noisette rose in his button-hole. His mother nearly had a fit as she descended from her carriage and beheld his costume ; but no one thought of wearing Pall Mall suits in Bluemere, and she trusted that Miss Janet might not be aware of the English etiquette concerning the clothes of parsons, who though they have been strictly enjoined to take no thought as to what they shall put on, are as particular about the shape of their collars and the brims of their hats as if they were young ladies in their first season.

However unorthodox might Bernard's coat and trousers have been, and that worldly and carnal noisette rose blooming so saucily in his button-hole, there was no fault to be found with his frank, smiling face and hospitable greeting, and he looked the very picture of a fine young Englishman as he welcomed his friends to Briarwood.

'How handsome Bernie is looking to-day,' whispered Laura to her mother. 'I have not seen him so bright and merry since Alice died.'

'Happier days are coming for him, thank heaven,' replied Mrs Freshfield, with a gush of premature gratitude, as she thought of the round-faced Bella, who, attired in a Stuart tartan, and a hat of purely Scotch manufacture, looked very much as if she had come out of a Noah's ark.

A cricket tent had been erected on the lawn, which sloped down to the copse where Phyllida first met Bernard, and from which even Miss Janet was obliged to confess that the view was like a peep of Paradise. The smooth turf ran for some distance green, pliant, and close shorn as a piece of emerald velvet, and the beds of flowers bloomed all round it like a belt of beauty and of sweetness. Shrubberies enclosed the garden on either side, shutting off the stables, the kennels, and the kitchen department. To the back was a pine grove to shelter the house from the east wind; beyond the copse in .front were richly pastured meadows where Bernard's Alderneys grazed, and his colts took their summer pastime. Look on which side you chose, Briarwood presented the picture of a well-ordered and well-kept English homestead. There was but one thing wanting there,— it was a Paradise without an Eve!

Mrs Freshfield whispered something of this kind to Miss Muckheep, as the ladies followed Mrs Garnett, the housekeeper, to the room which had been prepared for their temporary use.

'Not in here, Mrs Garnett,' she exclaimed, as the servant turned the handle of the principal bedroom door.

'Yes, madam, his reverence gave me orders it was to be so,' Mrs Garnett replied, as she ushered the party into a large bedroom, magnificently furnished in the French fashion with white and blue and gold.

'Dear me, how very peculiar,' remarked Mrs Freshfield, as soon as they were alone. 'This was poor, dear Alice's bedroom, Miss Janet, and my son has never occupied it since she was called away. I wonder what made him order it to be prepared for our use to-day! It is very flattering; don't you think so? I know it is not *everybody* whom Bernard would admit to *this* room, and it is a direct compliment to you and dear Miss Bella. How sweet she looks!'

'Mamma! mamma! who is that lovely girl?' exclaimed Laura, interrupting Mrs Freshfield's confidences, as the door re-opened to admit another party of guests. 'Oh, there is Mrs Pinner! it must be her cousin, Miss Moss!'

Phyllida, in a dress of some clear black stuff, made full and high to her throat, and which yet revealed the creamy fairness of her arms and shoulders—with a large Rembrandt hat upon her head, with a drooping black feather, and not a single ornament to clash with the perfect beauty of her features — did look pre-eminently lovely, and startled even her own sex with a first view of her charms. But she stood beside Mrs Pinner, silent and unsmiling; without a single glance that betokened knowledge of her own fairness: and Laura's *second* thought concerning her was, how sorrowful she looked for one so young.

'Is this your cousin, Mrs Pinner; please to introduce me,' she said quickly.

'Oh yes! certainly, Miss Freshfield, with pleasure. Her name is Phyllida Moss. It was so good of our dear minister to include her in his invitation. She actually didn't want to come, but I told her that would appear most ungrateful to Mr Freshfield and all of you.'

'I did not think there would be so many people,' interposed Phyllida, 'but it is quite a party.'

'I understand,' replied Laura, with a glance at the stranger's mourning ; 'and you have not been out much lately. But now you have come, Miss Moss, I hope you will enjoy yourself, and try and make friends with me. There are so few companionable young ladies in Bluemere.'

She had been smitten at first sight with the girl's pensive beauty, and was eager to know more of her. But Phyllida did not respond in like measure. Rather she smiled at Miss Freshfield's sudden enthusiasm as from the heights of a superior wisdom.

'I should have thought there were too many,' she replied, alluding to the young ladies, as she shook the dust from the skirt of her black dress.

'You overlooked my adjective,' said Laura merrily. 'But if you have finished arranging yourself, let us get out of this room. I can't bear it. It is the one in which my sister-in-law died.'

Phyllida looked round at the white and blue and gold adornments with interest.

'And does not your brother use it now?'

'No, never! He sleeps in a tiny room at the other side of the house.'

'How strange!'

'Do you think so? I should say how natural; what do we want with harbouring unpleasant memories? There is enough trouble in the world without that.'

'But when we have loved a person, can the memories be unpleasant?' demanded Phyllida.

Laura laughed.

'I am not to be drawn into a philosophical discussion to-day, Miss Moss. I have come here merely to enjoy myself; besides, I don't think my brother has ever cared for anybody in the way you mean. Let us go down and secure good seats for this famous collation.'

And the first view Bernard had of Phyllida that day was linked, arm in arm,

with his laughing sister Laura. The sight
warmed his heart as he hastened to greet
the two girls—and Phyllida's cheeks flushed
red as the heart of a damask rose when
she perceived him. The collation was
perfect ; and as Bernard kept on heaping
good things upon Miss Muckheep's plate,
his mother secretly wondered how he had
contrived to import aspic jelly and plover's
eggs, and truffles, and perigord pie to Bluemere, and why he had considered it worth
while to do her guests such honour as this,
when his native hams and home-made cakes
and strawberries and cream, had been considered sufficient provision for all former
parties at Briarfoot.

'Ech, mon!' exclaimed Miss Janet, as he
piled her plate with lobster salad, ' I'll nob-
but be sayin' but your jeelies and sallets,
and troofled tairkies air a' gude in their way,
but dinna forgit that they air but cairnal
pleesures, an' that in a few shairt yairs, we
shall a' be where seckit things air unknown.'

'Well, we have no actual proof of that, Miss Janet,' replied Bernard, laughing ; 'but if it *is* the case, let us make the most of them whilst we are here.'

'Eh, young man, but your puir feet air no in the reet pairth, if ye can airgue in sic a manner. I wish ye cou'd hair my gude brither the Laird o' Muckheep discoorse on seckit things. Ay, but he's a gude mon, and a Gawd - fearing, and treeds a' sic cairnal pleesures under his feet.'

'Why does your brother stay so much from home, Miss Janet?' inquired Laura ; 'why doesn't he live at Ballick-gallagas Castle with Bella and you?'

'Ay, but my dear, is it for the likes o' you and me to question the goin's and comin's of a pee-ous and Gawd - faering man like the Laird o' Muckheep? If he doesna' see fit to bide at Ballick-gallagas, ye may be sure 'tis the Laird's wairk as keepit him elsewheer. For my brither sheds the licht o' the garspel round him

wheerever he goes as a shinin' ray, and
when it is needed at the cairstle he will
be ca'd hame.'

' Where is the laird now ? ' asked Bernard,
wishing to be polite.

' I canna' say for cairtain, Mr Fraichfield,
but he's ay at Noo Yairk, or Cailifoornia
or the Valley o' Saicremeento, or any other
pairt wheer his blessed teachins air most
needed by the larist and ungardly souls,
wha' he was bairn to refairm.'

' What is the matter ? ' said Laura to her
neighbour, Phyllida Moss. The girl had
turned as white as marble, and the blue
veins on her forehead stood out like cords.

' Nothing, nothing ! only the day is rather
warm,' she answered.

Bernard glanced towards her anxiously.

' Take a glass of wine,' he said, pouring
out some sherry. ' You require it, Miss
Moss, you have turned quite pale.'

But she pushed the glass from her, and
turned her head the other way.

'You will not get Phyllida to touch wine,' remarked Miss Pinner. 'She is quite a teetotaller and cannot bear the sight of it. Perhaps you had better take a turn in the garden, my dear,' she added, 'if the ladies will excuse your absence. I am afraid the walk up here in the heat has been too much for you.'

But Phyllida refused to leave the table, declaring she was all right again, and sat out to the end of the meal, whilst Bernard kept looking at her white face anxiously, and blaming his own stupidity in not having thought of sending a carriage to convey her and Mrs Pinner to Briarwood. As soon as the collation was over, the old people disposed themselves on garden chairs and benches, whilst the young ones repaired to the lawn-tennis ground, and soon a merry party were sending the balls flying everywhere but over the net, whilst shouts of laughter accompanied each fresh failure or success. Bernard did not care to play himself; he was not by any means a croquet and worsted-work parson; but his young curate Frank Robinson enjoyed himself to the utmost, and tried hard to persuade Miss Moss to take a racket; but she shrunk visibly from the mere idea.

'Oh no!' she kept on saying, 'I could not run like that before everybody. Indeed, I couldn't. I should trip over my dress and fall, or do something dreadful; besides, I don't want to try; indeed, I don't!'

'Don't tease Miss Moss, Robinson,' interposed Bernard; 'the heat is trying her, and she would rather remain quiet.'

Mr Robinson departed with a bow, and Phyllida looked gratefully at the parson.

'Would you like to rest indoors till it is cooler?' continued Bernard. 'I want to show you my house before it grows dusk. Will you come?'

He held out his hand with a smile as he spoke, and she accompanied him without a word. Some remembrance of the last time

they had been alone together in the moonlight, leaning over Mrs Pinner's gate, was
doubtless in the mind of both, but neither
spoke of it. The hall and sitting-rooms of
Briarwood felt deliciously cool after the un-
sheltered heat of the garden, and Phyllida's
colour began to revive. It was a relief to
her to lose the sound of the loud laughing
and talking that was going on outside; to be
led by Bernard into one pretty shaded room
after another, and to be invited to repose
on the luxurious chairs and couches, seemed
like the peace and quiet of heaven after the
rattle of the world. She followed him first
to the drawing-room, which was quaintly
furnished in the Louis Quinze style, with
sateen of a pale pink colour, decorated with
little cupids and ribbons in blue, and had a
grand piano standing in one corner, and
mirrors framed in ebony and gold to match
the chairs and tables. Bernard wanted Phyllida to try the piano, but she shrank from
awakening the echoes in that empty house.

'Don't ask me,' she said, with evident repugnance. 'It would seem like sacrilege to sing to that piano. I guess it was her's, and I should fancy she was listening all the while, and reproaching me for daring to use her things.'

'It will be very unfortunate for me if every one holds your opinions,' said Bernard gravely, as he closed the piano lid. 'Is my house always to be a house of mourning, because my first venture turned out a failure ?'

But he did not ask her to sing again, and he led her quickly through the other apartments, until they reached the library, which was hung with purple velvet and furnished with old oak. Bernard's writing-table and chair stood on a Persian carpet at one end of the long room, and over the mantelpiece hung an oil painting of a girl, with a delicate face and soft braids of fair hair and a lapful of flowers. Phyllida guessed it was the portrait of the dead wife.

'I shall keep you a prisoner here,' said Bernard playfully, 'until you look yourself again. Come, take off your hat and lean back in that chair, it is my own particular lounge when I am lazy, and I know you will find it comfortable. Do you hear that sound ? It is my dogs baying to get loose ; it is about the time when the groom takes them out for exercise. I love to sit here and listen to their voices. They are company for me when I am alone.'

He threw open the window as he spoke, and leaned his arms upon the sill.

'Ah, Mrs Benson !' he exclaimed as he recognised a figure walking slowly through the grounds, 'what brings you here to-day ? '

'I came to see you, sir, but they told me you had company on the lawn, and so I was just taking my way home again.'

'But that was wrong of Mrs Garnett. She knows I am always at the service of my friends. Is anything the matter ? '

'Rachel's gone, sir,' replied the old woman, and as she advanced to the open window, Phyllida could see that the tears were coursing down her cheeks; 'she went this morning at seven o'clock, and her last words were a prayer and a blessing for you.'

'My poor friend,' said Bernard, as he took the woman's withered hand in his, 'I feel for you deeply. It must be very hard to bear, now it has come—though we expected it so long.'

'I would be the last to complain, sir. It was written she was to go, and I kept her longer than I had any reason to hope. And, thanks to your goodness, my poor Rachel was ready for her change when it did come.'

'Say, rather, thanks to the goodness of God, Mrs Benson,' corrected the parson gently.

'No, sir, I can't unsay my words. I know of course that it was the goodness of God as enabled you to do it—so 'twould be if you gave a crust to a starving creature ; but *you'd* give it all the same, and if it hadn't been for your patience and long-suffering and prayers, my poor Rachel would have left this world as careless as she lived in it. It's all owing to you, sir, as I can believe and trust that she's in glory now.'

' But you mustn't say such things, Mrs Benson ; indeed you mustn't,' replied Bernard, visibly disturbed by the old woman's laudation. ' I did nothing more for your daughter than any other man would have done under the circumstances—Mr Robinson for instance, or Mr Blackett of Riversdale, or any other clergyman.'

' Why didn't Mr Robinson do it, then ?' demanded the mother shortly. ' You know it isn't the visiting nor the reading nor the teaching I speak of, sir. It's the Christian love you give my poor child— and the sympathy, and the prayers you prayed for her at home. I know you did

now, so it's no use denying it—that broke
down all the pride in her poor heart. And
the last words she said to me was, " Am
I going, mother? Then may God bless
Mr Freshfield for ever and ever." Them
was my Rachel's last words, sir,' continued
the woman, wiping her eyes, 'and I'll
never forget them nor you, till the grave
closes over myself.'

Bernard Freshfield looked as stupid and
conscious during this harangue as though
he had been detected in a crime. His fair
cheeks crimsoned like those of a woman's,
and he did not once glance in the direction of his guest.

'Mrs Benson,' he said, quietly ignoring
all that had passed, 'don't go home until
you have had some refreshment. Go to
Garnett's room and get a glass of wine or
a cup of her good tea. You are not fit to
undertake the walk back without—'

'No, sir, don't ask me. I couldn't
touch bit nor sup, nor would I have

come up to-day if I'd known you were
engaged. But she looks beautiful, sir—so
peaceful and happy—and you'll come and
see her, wont you, before she's screwed
down ? I know she'd like to think you did.'

'I will come the first thing to-morrow
morning, Mrs Benson.'

'God bless you, sir! you've been more
like an angel than a human being to us. And
you'll bury her, too, sir. Won't you?'

'Of course, I will!'

'Ah! it's a shame for every one to come
a troubling you as we do, when you've
had so many troubles of your own to
bear. There's never a burying in Bluemere, but every one on us thinks of the
day when you laid your sweet lady under
the ground. But you trampled down your
own griefs for our sakes, and may the
Lord, in His infinite mercy, send you the
happiness as you deserve at last. That
was Rachel's prayer, sir, and it is mine
as well.'

'Amen,' said Bernard solemnly; and he leaned out of the window and watched the old woman's figure till it was out of sight.

When he turned to Phyllida again, it was with half an apology that their *tête-à-tête* should have been interrupted by a matter of parochial interest.

'These poor people are absurdly enthusiastic,' he observed, 'and fond of making mountains out of mole hills.'

But as he looked at the girl leaning back in the purple velvet arm-chair, with her hair lying somewhat loosely on the cushion, and her large eyes fixed upon the sky, he saw that there were tears upon her cheek.

'Phyllida! — Miss Moss — what is this? Are you ill again? Let me fetch you some iced water.' But all the answer she gave him was to catch his hand impulsively between her own, whilst she exclaimed, 'How good you are! How very good you are!'

'Indeed, *indeed,* I am not. You must not think so. You distress me by the idea.'

'Why do you try to hide it?' cried Phyllida, 'to live such a life as you do; what can be better? To teach people how to be good; to turn their thoughts away from this wicked, heartless world and give them the blessed hope that there will be another, where we can begin life over again, and forget all the misery we endured in this?'

'Can you doubt it? Have you ever doubted it?' he said tenderly.

'Thousands and thousands of times. I have always doubted it. I do so now. What have I seen or heard to make me believe? My experience is, that the wicked succeed and the good are miserable; that our prayers go out upon the empty air, and come back to us unanswered; that the young and happy die, and those who long for death live on for ever. And no one has ever tried to teach me otherwise.'

Bernard looked very grave, for some of the girl's arguments were unanswerable, and he knew that neither Church nor Bible held the key to them. There is but one thing that reconciles the trials of this world with the belief in the next—the love, human and divine, that sanctifies and alleviates and shares the first, and will endure unto the second ; and Phyllida knew no such love.

' If I had been taught like your Alice,' she went on vehemently ; ' if I had had a friend and a guide like her, I might have been a different creature with a different mind; and yet *she*, who had everything in this world, died and left it, whilst I live on. Oh, how could she—how *could* she die,' continued Phyllida, raising her wet eyes to the portrait, ' with so much goodness and happiness around her ? Had she no energy—no courage ? The very thought of what I had to leave behind me would have *made* me live ! '

' Do you consider, then, that Alice's lot

was such a happy one?' asked Bernard softly.

'How could it have been happier? You, who love and pray for even the poor of your parish, who are no relations to you, would not have done less for the wife of your bosom.'

'I hope not,' he replied. 'Alice was too good and pure to need my teaching; but my sympathy and counsel were always hers to claim.'

'And yet she *died*,' said Phyllida.

'God called her,' said Bernard, 'and when His call comes it must be obeyed. If love and care could have kept her here she would have remained; but she was quite content to go—contented, obedient, and resigned.'

'I should not have been.'

The words left Phyllida's lips almost unintentionally, but Bernard heard them, and the deep flush of passion mounted to his face. He forgot everything—their slight acquaintance, his staid profession, his utter ignorance of her antecedents—and remembered only that he was a man.

'Phyllida,' he exclaimed in a low trembling voice, 'is it possible you envy her? Speak to me; don't keep me in suspense. You must have guessed what I feel for you. From the moment we met I knew that I and my fate had come together. Say you will fill her place. No, no! what am I dreaming of? Say rather you will fill the place in my heart that has never yet been occupied—that has been waiting for your image, my darling and my wife.'

He pressed upon her as he spoke; he would have taken her in his arms then and there, but Phyllida sprang from her seat and kept him off with both her hands.

'No! no! What are you thinking of? You must be *mad! I* your wife—*I*—the wife of a man whose life is spent in doing good! Oh! you do not know me—your eyes are blinded—you will be terribly sorry for all this to-morrow.'

Bernard stopped short, and put his hands to his head as if bewildered.

'You are talking reasonably, I suppose,' he said. 'Let me try and answer your words. I do not know you! Not if you count by weeks or months, perhaps—but love needs no such knowledge. I read your heart instinctively the first hour we met, and years could not increase the sympathy nor interest I feel in you. I do not know your parentage, nor antecedents, nor your character, perhaps—but I do not want to know them. All I want is, to be one with you henceforward. You have felt sorrow— I want to comfort you. You need instruc- tion—I want to teach you. You have no clear hope of nor belief in a merciful Creator and a blissful hereafter—I want to give them you. I want to make you happy and hopeful and good, by infusing my life in yours, and showing you that love is the great regenerator of the world. In one word, Phyllida, I love you ! I cannot tell why— I do not know how. I know only that you must be mine, or I will go through life unmated. Come to me, darling. See, how open my arms are to receive you ! Come, and find your rest and refuge here ! '

But she shrank still farther from him, reiterating, ' I cannot—I cannot. Oh, how I wish I could ! '

' Child ! do you love me ? '

' I do not know ! I am so bewildered I cannot tell—only I would go to you with perfect confidence as I am.'

' And I would hold you safe against the world by the force of my passion ! What is it that comes between us, then ? Is there any obstacle to our marriage ? '

She shook her head decidedly.

' Does it exist in your imagination only ? '

' I am not worthy.'

Bernard sighed, but remained steadfast.

'I do not ask your confidence. Some day when you are my wife you will give it me without asking. Only—granted that you are right—it makes no difference to my love. You shall but have the larger, fuller need of it to absolve you from your sin. I repeat I love you!'

'Oh, Mr Freshfield! It must not, cannot be! You have only seen me three times altogether!'

'Three times or three hundred times are all the same to me! The more I see of you perhaps, the more I shall esteem you, but esteem is not love. As love is a free gift from God to man, so is it free from man to woman. I do not want to bargain with you for an exchange for my love. It is your's without limit or restraint, because I cannot help giving it to you.'

'And neither can I help loving you. Heaven have mercy on me!' cried Phyllida, with a burst of tears. But Freshfield would not let them flow. He took her hands from before her face and kissed her passionately.

'My love—my darling—my true wife! Say you will come to me!' he exclaimed, as he held her in his arms.

'I must not—I cannot! Oh, do not ask me!'

'You have confessed your love for me, and I will not let you take it back again. Only for the sake of Bluemere I will give you time. How soon may I tell the world that you are mine.'

'I am not! I will not let you say so! But I will give you my decision in a month. And before that time you will regret you ever asked for it.'

'In a month! A long, drawn-out, weary month! Think of the days and nights of suspense that I shall suffer! Oh, my love! make it less than a month.'

'I cannot! It is far too short a period. I must have time to consider and decide what is right for me to do.'

'You might think and consider for twice two hundred months,' said Bernard, 'but at the end of that time, Phyllida, you would be mine. It is fate—do not try to battle with it, for it will be useless. God has given you to me, and you are mine; mine for time and for eternity.'

He held her from him for a few moments, gazing at her as though he were drinking in every detail of her beauty; then, almost roughly, he kissed her upon brow and lips and bosom, and put her away from him.

Phyllida stood where he had left her, too much overcome to speak or move, whilst Bernard took two or three hasty strides up and down the room.

When he returned to her side, he was the courteous, smiling host of an hour before.

'Shall we go back to the garden?' he said, drawing her arm through his own. 'I think you are rested now, and will enjoy the cool evening amongst my beautiful flowers.'

But before they passed out of the library he stopped once more and gazed in her face.

'My wife,' he said, with a look of ineffable tenderness, 'my true wife found at last! Thank God! thank God!'

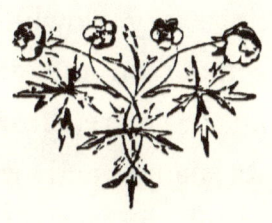

CHAPTER VI.

T was about five or six days after that eventful party at Briarwood that Miss Annie Warren met Phyllida, walking very slowly and steadily, with her eyes fixed on the ground, beside the broad lake or mere, from which the village took its name, and which was on the road to one of the outlying districts of the parish. Phyllida had chosen that path, because she thought it unlikely she should meet Mr Freshfield there. She knew nothing of the patch of common beyond, and his parishioners who lived upon it. She had been hiding from him ever since that passionate scene in the library in which he had claimed her as his, whether she would or not ; and he was too delicate to break voluntarily on her seclusion, although he had paid more than one visit to Mrs Pinner, in hopes of seeing her. His mother and sister also had called upon Phyllida, and Laura had been disappointed on that occasion by Miss Moss's absence ; but Mrs Pinner had no idea where she was gone, although she had but run to hide herself amongst the cabbages at the back of the house, as soon as she heard the carriage wheels. She was shy in fact of meeting any of the family, until the mighty question Bernard had raised between them should be settled, and all day long she walked or sat about in the loneliest places she could find, asking herself, ' What *shall* I do ? What shall I do ? '

Miss Warren could not comprehend such shyness. Had she been placed in the position of Phyllida, all the parish would have been acquainted with the fact twelve hours

N

after. She could only imagine, therefore, that this melancholy air was put on to curry favour with the parson ; perhaps even to induce him to employ her in the parish, which her presence on the road to Brick Common seemed to verify. Miss Annie was in a spiteful mood that day, she had been so ever since the party to which she had received no invitation, and Miss Moss seemed a fit subject to vent it upon.

'You here?' she exclaimed with well-acted surprise as she came up with Phyllida. She had seen and recognised her full three minutes before. 'I *am* surprised. What on earth can *you* be doing at Brick Common ?'

'What are you doing here yourself?' retorted Phyllida.

'Oh! *I* am at my parish work, of course. *My* hands are full from morning till night ; thanks to the entire confidence reposed in me by our dear minister. He gives Mr Robinson his instructions daily, but he never thinks of interfering with anything I may do. He has known me and my method too long, you see. And as for giving me a rival to share my parochial duties, I believe he would as soon think of cutting off his right hand,' continued Miss Warren, with a laugh that was intended to be the height of confidence. 'For he knows that I should resign my position at once, and he would lose my services altogether.'

'I should think you need have no fear of any one wishing to supplant you, Miss Warren. Attending to old men and women cannot be very pleasant work.'

'Not if you look at it in a *worldly* light; certainly not,' replied Miss Warren, severely, 'but why should I talk to you on the subject? The wisest words fall unheeded on the ears as yet unstopped by grace. And what sort of party did you have at Briarwood last Tuesday? I was so busy, I had no time to come.'

'Were you asked?' demanded Phyllida

innocently. Miss Warren grew very red, but stood to her ground.

'It will be a strange day, indeed, when there are parties given at Briarwood, to which I am *not* asked,' she said; 'but everybody in Bluemere is talking of the extraordinary manner in which the invitations for this one were sent out. All Mr Freshfield's *dearest* and *oldest* friends omitted, and *perfect strangers* of whom he knew nothing, asked instead. Whoever counselled him, did very unwisely. It has created quite a scandal in Bluemere.'

'But perhaps it was Mr Freshfield's own wish, Miss Warren. The society of strangers makes a pleasant change sometimes, in a dull place like this.'

'You don't know Mr Freshfield, or you would not say so—he is not the man to neglect those who have been with him through all his trouble. I expect the invitations were left to his mother and sister, and that old lady Miss Muckheep

has got a finger in the pie. Everybody
says she is mad, and Laura Freshfield is
not much better. She doesn't care with
whom she associates ; she actually walked
straight through the village the other day
on the arm of a Roman Catholic.'

' How dreadful !' cried Phyllida, laughing.

' Ah ! you may laugh, Miss Moss, but
we in Bluemere have been taught to think
differently from yourself ; and our minister
is like a beacon set on a hill—he can do
nothing that is not known and commented
on far and wide. I can tell you that poor
dear Alice hardly dared do anything, until
she knew what Bluemere would think of
it. I remember once her taking a feather
out of her hat, because some one said that
it looked too gay—a minister's wife cannot
be too particular, nor a minister in the
choice of his friends. But *some* people
will push their way anywhere. What did
you do at Briarwood ?' continued Miss
Annie, who was dying to hear all about it.

'Can't you ask somebody else, Miss Warren, since you know every one in Bluemere? *I* am a stranger here, remember! Besides, I was not well on that day, and did less than any one else.'

Something in the girl's look and tone warned Miss Warren she had said enough.

'Of course I can,' she replied, jerking the heavy basket on her arm. 'I can ask Mr Freshfield himself for that matter, as I am just going to meet him. Good-bye, Miss Moss. I wouldn't keep on this road if I were you—for Farmer Green's bull is allowed to roam about these meadows at his will, and he is dangerous with strangers.'

'Thank you; but I am not afraid of bulls,' said Phyllida, as her companion left her to herself. But as soon as Miss Warren was out of sight, she *did* quicken her steps, though it was not from fear of Farmer Green's bull. 'I cannot meet *him*,' she thought to herself; 'he will renew that subject, and I shall not know what to tell

him. That woman is right—with all her
spite and jealousy, she speaks the truth.
A minister is like a beacon set on a
hill. He cannot lower himself without
lowering his profession. Oh, I must not
—I *must not* do as he asks me. It
would be so sweet to feel myself safe
and good with him, but I am unworthy
of it, and if he knew me as I am, he
would not press me to share his happy
home. I *love him,*' she continued, grind-
ing her pretty teeth together, ' I feel I
love him for all his goodness to me and
every one. He is like an angel from
heaven to me, and so I must not marry
him. Oh, I will not—I will not. I
will run away, where he shall never find
me again. I will go back to my old
life—I will do anything except tell him
the truth. But it is hard—hard. Why
was I created to be different from other
women ? Why should I be unfit to be
a pure and happy wife and mother ?

Why must *I*, who long so much to be good and innocent and free from blame, refuse the very means which would make me so ? I could love him a thousand times better than that pale-faced, stupid-looking girl who was his wife ; but she would have borne his contempt more quietly than I could. For I would *kill* him before I would see his love change to hatred or indifference. Oh, how I wish I had never met him. I wish I had the courage to throw myself to the bottom of that lake and forget everything that has ever happened to me.'

She leaned far over the water as these thoughts · passed through her mind, and looked down into its placid depths. They were dark but clear as a mirror, and as Phyllida gazed at her own reflection, another face appeared beside her's, smiling eagerly. It was that of Bernard Freshfield. She started as if she had been shot.

' Take care, my love !' he exclaimed

anxiously; 'these banks are very steep and slippery, and unless you can swim, I would not answer for your reappearance after a submersion in the Blue Mere. Of what were you thinking, Phyllida, that my sudden apparition should make you start so violently?'

The answer was very different from what he expected.

'I was thinking how much trouble it would save me, to be lying asleep for ever down there.'

'Haven't I already told you that is wrong?' he answered gravely; 'besides, it is cruel to me. How do you think *I* should feel now if your dear eyes and mouth were closed to me for ever. Would you trample down my new-found happiness with the memories of another coffin and another grave?'

'It is for *your* sake I would do it,' cried Phyllida passionately, 'that you might forget you had ever seen or heard me·

Oh, Mr Freshfield, you must never speak to me again as you did last Tuesday. It is quite impossible. It can never be. You lower yourself by the mere idea.'

'That is *my* business, is it not?' said Bernard Freshfield; 'and if I tell you that I feel lifted up to the very heights of heaven by the feeling you have excited in me, how can you gainsay my words? Phyllida,' he continued, coming closer to her, 'you have given me the grandest gift that one mortal can give to another—you have taught me how to love. Henceforward I am greater, nearer to God, for the love I bear you, and I cannot, will not, give it up.'

'Think of your mother—your sister,' she murmured. 'Think of the people of Blue-mere, and what they will say to such a folly on your part.'

His lip slightly curled.

'How little you know me, child, to ima-

gine that the opinions of the world would
sway my resolve! How little you must
comprehend the depth of the passion I
have conceived for you—unsought, unwished-
for, but overwhelming, if you think that
ten thousand relations or friends could stand
in the way of its accomplishment! I love
you, as man loves woman only once; and
I will hold you against the world. Don't
wound me by saying you cannot understand it.'

The girl turned suddenly and threw herself into his arms.

' I *do* understand it! Bernard, I understand it far better than you think. If you
must have me, then, if it be necessary to
your happiness to call me yours, take me!
Make me your slave, your servant, what
you will! I will work for you in secret,
and love you in secret, and be grateful to
you for the least sign that tells me you
are happy in my love. But don't make
me your wife, for I am not worthy.'

The young man's arms, which had been clasped tightly round her supple form, fell from her like failing reeds.

'What!' he exclaimed, '*mine* and yet not my wife? Phyllida, do you know what you are saying?'

'Oh, it would be far better so,' she went on wildly. 'You have told me several times that marriage should be of the heart, and not dependent upon formal ties. Take me then for your true wife—if you will! I *will* be true to you, Bernard, in thought and word and deed; and I will never, never ask for more than you may choose to give me. But don't marry me. I have ·seen what marriage means. A gradual but sure decay of feeling and respect and courtesy. I could not bear that from you. The contempt of a good man would be my ruin. You shall not pull yourself down for my sake. It were better, far better, that I were lying in the waters of the mere.'

He put his arms about her then, and drew her forcibly from the spot. He seemed to be afraid lest she should really cast herself headlong in the lake.

'Listen to me, dear,' he said tenderly. 'I have told you how I love you. Now, I tell you that I would rather see you dead than slay your purity with my own hand.'

'And you despise me for proposing it.'

'Not so. If you *could* be dearer to me than you have already grown, this noble sacrifice of self would make you so. I know what a woman must feel before she consents to give up all that makes life valuable to her for the sake of a man. I am glad you said it, because it proves how much you love me, but you must never say it again. My wife must be above suspicion.'

'And of me you know—nothing.'

'Oh, don't say that! Has not my love taught me what you are? Have I not read the purity of your feelings—the warmth of your heart—the earnest desires you entertain for goodness and virtue. It is in you, Phyllida, to become all that is most honourable and good, and with me (and the help of God), you shall attain it.'

'I almost think I could,' she answered, weeping.

'And I am sure of it! Tell me, now, may I not claim your promise to be my wife?'

'No, no! not yet. You know we settled that we were to take a month's consideration.'

'*You* did,' he answered, smiling. 'Well then, sweetheart, I will not worry you; but there is but one answer that I will accept at the end of that time. And now I must leave you, for I was on my way to Brick Common. This has been a dreary week to me without your presence, but it is so many days nearer the moment when I shall claim you for my own. Good-bye, good-bye.'

He went away smiling till he was out of

sight, but her mind was full of perplexity and fear. The old question came to the surface, and Phyllida went on her way, wringing her hands and crying, 'What *shall* I do?'

When she reached home the point seemed solved for her. Mrs Pinner, like many another charitable Christian, had benevolently invited Phyllida to Bluemere, more for her own sake than that of the girl.

She had thought it would be so pleasant to have some one to run messages for her, and do needlework, and generally undertake the housekeeping. And when Miss Moss failed to display any domestic proclivities whatever, and preferred roaming about the meadows with a volume of Shakspeare in her hand, to washing and combing Mrs Pinner's pet poodle Tiny, or accompanying her to the Dorcas meeting, held once a week under the supervision of Miss Warren, her cousin began to wish she had never asked her to Bluemere. But she had a sister, a

Mrs Penfold, also a widow, who lived at a little town on the sea coast, called Gatehead, where she made her livelihood by letting furnished lodgings. As soon, therefore, as Mrs Pinner found that Phyllida was likely to prove only an encumbrance to herself, she wrote the most laudatory accounts of her beauty and goodness to her sister Penfold, in hopes that lady would offer to take her off her hands; and since a young dependant relation, who is willing to make herself generally useful, is quite as desirable an inmate of a sea-side lodging house as of a cottage in the country, the bait took, and Mrs Penfold was just as eager to get Phyllida to Gatehead as Mrs Pinner had been to induce her to visit Bluemere.

And this intelligence Mrs Pinner made known to her over the tea-table, where she appeared that evening, white, heavy-eyed, and languid.

'Why, bless my soul, Phyllida!' exclaimed

her cousin, and with reason, 'how ill you
look. You have been sitting out in that
blazing sun again without anything on your
head. You will have a sunstroke some day
if you don't take more care of yourself.'

'I have been in the shade all the afternoon,' was Phyllida's quiet answer.

'I have just received a letter from my
sister, Maria Penfold. Such a nice letter,'
continued Mrs Pinner. 'Maria is an excellent creature, one of the salt of the earth,
and Gatehead is the prettiest sea-side place
you ever saw.'

'Cousin Penfold lets lodgings there,
doesn't she?' inquired Phyllida, who saw
no sin in letting lodgings. But Mrs Pinner
had some particles of the old man still
clinging to her, and one weakness which
she shared with the carnal-minded was a
false shame with respect to the occupation
of her poorer relation.

Mr Pinner and Mr Penfold had been
equal in point of station in this world, but

one had succeeded in business and the other had failed ; hence Mr Pinner's widow was a lady in comfortable circumstances in Bluemere, and Mr Penfold's was a lodging-house keeper in Gatehead, and the lady of Bluemere was very much ashamed of the fact. It was some time before she could collect her thoughts to answer suitably to her cousin's straightforward question.

'Well, my dear,' she said at last, 'she certainly *does* in a measure, but you will agree with me that it is as well not to mention it.'

'But it isn't *wrong*,' quoth Phyllida.

'*Wrong!* I should hope not, indeed,' replied Mrs Pinner, with a jerk of her head. 'It would be a sad day when any one connected with me by blood did anything that was *wrong*. Still, to let lodgings is not an occupation to which any of my father's daughters ever thought to come down, and therefore I have never said anything about it to my friends in Bluemere.

' I see! You are ashamed of cousin Penfold,' said Phyllida boldly.

' Phyllida, you really do have the most extraordinary ideas! How *could* I be ashamed of my own sister,—born of the same good parents as myself, and walking side by side with me in the light of the truth to heaven ? Have I not already told you what an excellent creature is Maria? And she does not exactly let lodgings either. Her house is too large for her, for she is childless like myself, and an old gentleman and lady occupy the first and second floors. They are highly respectable both of them, and have been living with Maria for years past, so you see it is not like being a common lodging-house keeper to share her very comfortable home with them.'

' I see that cousin Penfold must be a nice woman, or they wouldn't have stayed with her so long. I wonder if she would be good to me too, and find me some occupation in Gatehead. For I am tired of this idle life, cousin Pinner, and it is time I did something to support myself.'

This was the very opening Mrs Pinner required.

'How strange you should say so, Phyllida, for Maria is most anxious to make your acquaintance. I will read you what she writes, "Do you think Phyllida Moss could be persuaded to pay me a visit at Gatehead? I remember her mother as a girl, though you do not, and should be glad to know her daughter. The sea-side is charming just now. Our little season has just commenced, and Gatehead is as full as it can be. If our young cousin would like to spend a few weeks with me, tell her to come before the fine weather is over." There,' continued Mrs Pinner folding up her letter, 'you see what Maria says on the matter, and you can make your own choice.'

But she was hardly prepared for the energy with which Phyllida entered into the new scheme.

'I will go at once,' she said. 'I shall enjoy it above all things; and I am sure the sea will do me good. How far is Gatehead from here, cousin Pinner, and can I start to-morrow?'

'You seem to be in a tremendous hurry to go,' replied Mrs Pinner, who, though she wanted to get rid of her visitor, was not over pleased at her alacrity to leave. 'Gatehead is half-a-day's journey from Bluemere, and I shall have to borrow a time-table from the rectory before I can tell you at what hours the trains leave Westertown.'

'Don't think me ungrateful,' said Phyllida, as she took the old lady's hand; 'I am afraid I have been a great bother to you since I came here, and you have been very patient with me. Only—I have had trouble (as you know) and it doesn't seem to lessen, and I think the sooner I set to work the sooner I shall learn to overcome it.'

'Don't say any more, my dear,' replied

Mrs Pinner; 'I'm too old to be a good companion for you, and you don't seem to have taken to the young ladies of Bluemere—but you will have gayer scenes and perhaps gayer friends in Gatehead; for though my sister Maria has been trained in the ways of grace, I sometimes fear that her heart still inclines to carnal pleasures and company.'

Phyllida heaved a sigh of thanksgiving on the spot. But she had another petition to proffer.

'You wont send to the rectory for the time-table, will you, cousin Pinner?'

'Why not, my dear? Our dear minister is always but too ready to share his good gifts with his people!'

'Yes; but I don't want Mr Freshfield to hear that I am going to Gatehead. I think, perhaps—at least, I feel almost sure—that (in his capacity as minister, you know) he might consider it his duty to urge me to remain in Bluemere and try and live down any troubles with parish work, and so forth.'

'But, my dear,' commenced Mrs Pinner, who was alarmed at this prospect of recantation, 'Mr Freshfield could hardly take the parish work out of Miss Warren's hands—she does everything in that way, you know—it would be a positive insult to her! And where am I to borrow a time-table except from him? We travel so little from Bluemere.'

'Perhaps Miss Warren may have one,' suggested Phyllida.

'She may. That is a happy idea on your part, for her brother lives in London, and is often here on a visit. Shall I send Mary over to ask her?'

'Yes, cousin Pinner; and say why you want it. Miss Warren will not try to prevent my leaving Bluemere—I am sure of that.'

And the upshot of this conversation was, that Phyllida Moss and her box were driven to Westertown the very next day; and she had reached her destination of Gatehead before her lover was aware that she no longer breathed the same air as himself.

It was the evening after her departure that he came sauntering up Mrs Pinner's garden path, hoping to catch the ladies over their frugal tea. But Mrs Pinner sat alone at the radish-crowned board.

'Is Miss Moss still roaming?' he asked pleasantly, as he entered the little room. 'What an inquisitive young lady she is. I do not believe that there is a nook or corner of Bluemere that she has not explored. She is a thorough lover of the country.'

'Have you not heard that my cousin has left me, Mr Freshfield? She went to my sister's at Gatehead yesterday,' replied Mrs Pinner, on whom Phyllida had laid no embargo as to concealing her destination. For she believed that once out of Bluemere, she should at least be allowed as much time as

she chose, in which to make up her mind
respecting Bernard Freshfield, for a parson
(so she imagined) must remain at his post
of duty until she saw fit to rejoin him.
When Mrs Pinner made her announcement
to Bernard, his face grew as pale as ashes.
She said afterwards (when circumstances
had thrown their light upon his behaviour)
that she guessed the truth from merely looking at him. But that was not the case. At
the moment she only thought that he was ill,
or vexed at letting a probable convert slip
through his fingers.

'Dear me, Mr Freshfield,' she exclaimed,
'you look quite poorly. Do sit down and
have a cup of tea. Yes, Phyllida went off
to my sister Penfold's yesterday. It was
rather a surprise to me, as you may imagine,
for I had invited her to stay with me over the
winter, but I am afraid our ways didn't suit
her. She's rather flighty, and I have been
brought up, as you know, in the strictest
principles, and used to refer all my doings

to the Throne of Grace, and it did not suit the girl. Two cannot walk together, as we know, except they be agreed. And the ways of the righteous are as a stumbling-block to the ungodly.'

' No, no tea, thank you,' the parson said in rather a strange voice, as he put back the cup she offered him. ' ' To Gatehead, did you say ? '

' Yes, to my sister Maria. She lives in Shirland Villas, Gatehead, and was kind enough to invite the girl to stay with her. Directly Phyllida received the invitation, she jumped at it—ungratefully, I cannot but say—and insisted upon going off the very next day. I wished her to consult you upon the matter, Mr Freshfield, for, as I said, what greater privilege can we have than a minister's advice ; but she is a wrong-headed creature, and she wouldn't hear of it. She said you'd keep her here, and set her about parish work. Such nonsense ! But I've often thought that Phyllida is a

little wanting. I hope my sister Penfold
may make more of her than I did. And you
wont take any tea then, Mr Freshfield?'

'No, thanks,' he stammered; and then
rising suddenly, 'I must go on to Blue
Mount. I have something of importance
to tell my mother,' and before his hostess
could remonstrate with him he was gone.

'So strange, my dear,' as she observed
to Annie Warren somewhat later, 'to leave
me all alone in that way, and when I was
just in the humour to enjoy a little company! Not like a minister, I must say;
but still, as he went to Blue Mount, I suppose I must not complain. He said he
had something of importance to tell his
mother. I wonder what it can be.'

If Mrs Pinner could have followed her
minister to Blue Mount, she would have
been still more astonished. He entered
Mrs Freshfield's private sitting-room with
troubled eyes and ruffled hair, looking more
like a man walking in his sleep than an

animate being, and flung himself upon the nearest seat.   The old lady was alone, occupied with her eternal knitting.

'Good heavens! Bernard,' she exclaimed, as she looked up at him over her spectacles, 'what is the matter?'

'Nothing,' he said, starting.   'Do I look as if there were.   It is this diabolical heat.'

'*Bernard!*' cried Mrs Freshfield.

'I beg your pardon, mother, I mean it is the heat that has upset me.   I don't feel at all well to-day.   It's enough to make any man seedy, to tramp over a parish from morning till night, in such sun as this.'

'You should wear a "solar topee,"' remarked his mother practically.

'I want change—that is the truth—and I intend to take it.   Robinson can do the work of Bluemere very well for a few weeks by himself.   You know, mother, that I have not left the parish since my wife died.'

'No, my dear, you have not; and a most excellent opportunity presents itself at present. Dear Miss Janet was lamenting only yesterday that Dr Felinus was not here to accompany her and that sweet Bella back to Scotland. What would be more charming than for you to offer these two estimable ladies your escort? You would get a thorough change in the bracing air of Scotland, and see something of the beauties of that delightful country. Bernard, it is a most happy idea on your part; and if you are put to any extra expenses in the matter, of course I will defray them.'

'What! to go journeying about the country with that old woman? No, by Jove! I won't.'

'*Bernard,*' again exclaimed his mother, in a tone of horror, '*what* has come to you this evening?'

'I don't know, I'm sure,' replied the young man, passing his hand wearily over his brow. 'I am out of temper, I suppose, or out of sorts. Anyway, I can't be the Miss Muckheeps' escort. I must be free and alone, and I must start at once.'

'You surely will not leave Bluemere whilst my friends remain with me, Bernard? Think how strange it will appear, and what every one will say about it!'

'What do I care for what people *say?*' he exclaimed impetuously. 'The Muckheeps are no friends of mine, and never will be. Don't worry me on the subject, mother, for I came to say good-bye to you, and I shall start to-morrow.'

'Oh, this is terribly sudden! What can be the reason of it?' cried Mrs Freshfield. 'It is not customary for a minister to desert his flock in this way at a moment's warning.'

'My flock will be well provided for, or I should not leave it. The shepherd wants most looking after at present.'

'And where are you going, Bernard?'

demanded Mrs Freshfield in a solemn voice.

'I cannot tell you. I am not sure if I quite know myself; but you shall hear from me as soon as possible, and perhaps I may be able to tell you the reason of my determination.'

Mrs Freshfield only shook her head in sorrowful protest against such vicarious doings.

'Well, good-bye, mother,' said Bernard, rising. 'I don't want to go into the drawing-room, nor to see Laura nor anybody. I am not fit for any company but my own to-night. Tell them of my determination, and let them put what interpretation upon it they choose. It is hard if a man, who works as much as I do, cannot take a few weeks' relaxation without publishing his reasons to the world. I *wish it*, and I should think that ought to be sufficient.

And so saying, Bernard Freshfield turned on his heel, and with the same fretful despondent look upon his face, left the room. Such is the power that the thwarting of his fleshly inclinations may produce, even upon a man proverbially even-tempered, pious, and self-sacrificing!

END OF VOL. I.

COLSTON AND SON, PRINTERS, EDINBURGH.

www.ingramcontent.com/pod-product-compliance
Lightning Source LLC
Chambersburg PA
CBHW030116030726
47498CB00007B/2403